I0621878

The Pleasures Collection
Book Three

SEDUCTIVE PLEASURES

a novel

by
Natasha Simmons

Seductive Pleasures

ISBN-13: 978-0988299443
ISBN-10: 0988299445

Published by Thomas Publishing

Cover photography provided by: Michele Williamson

Author photo provided by: K.S. Photography

Inspiration is gifted. Thank you, Phil.

With all my love,

N.S.

Seductive Pleasures

Seduction tastes like the thrill of a rollercoaster ride dipped in honey.

Prologue

Sweet Gardenias

The day came as he knew it would. He remembered the gardenias smelling especially sweet that morning from the open window above the kitchen sink. She loved gardenias and he picked one for her each day they were in full bloom. No matter how weak she was or how much her hands trembled, she always picked it up and held it to her nose before replacing it in the tiny vase to take the small mountain of pills piled next to her breakfast plate.

"Find a girl that smells as sweet as this flower, Ethan and you will have a keeper." She would say.

"Yea Ma, but these give me a headache." Ethan always replied.

"That's when you know you've picked the right one." She countered with a wink.

Why in the world would he want a woman around that would give him a headache all the time? One day, to distract her when she was beating him badly in Scrabble, he asked.

She looked up at him with knowing eyes, but answered him anyway.

"She will be the one who challenges you and also the one who'll give you the most excitement." She took a slow deep breath before she continued. "She will be the one who hides pieces of herself in tiny crevices of your mind."

Ethan frowned, not understanding what she meant. She simply smiled and said, "You will never forget her." Then she lifted her fragile slender finger and pointed at him. "She will be the one worth keeping, Ethan."

The morning started no differently than any other. Ethan's alarm sounded at six-thirty and by seven-thirty he was showered, dressed and had breakfast prepared and plated for his mother. As he carried the tray in to her, he wondered how she could stand the strong aroma of the flower.

The gardenia went untouched *that* morning.

Four days passed while the arrangements were made and everyone complimented him on how well he was holding up. They said she would have been proud of him for not being sad, that she was in a better place.

Why do people say things like that?

How could he not be sad? She was his mother—his family. What would he do without her?

For three years she slipped farther and farther away and for three years the doctors told him to be prepared—be ready for when the day would come that she would slip away from him forever.

Dozens of people came to offer condolences and Ethan found himself consoling *them* instead of the other way around. He let no one help him make arrangements, handpicked every flower, her clothes, even the wig she wore because the poisons used to treat her, killed all of her hair follicles. He took care of all the details to bury his mother.

Most arrangements were made more than a year before, but emotionally there is really nothing to be done ahead of time to prepare for losing a loved one. However, he was strong and thankful for all the love his adopted mother had given him. He'd hated seeing her in pain and like many people said to him, he knew she was in a better place than the constant pain wracking her body from the cancer setting out to destroy it.

Ethan Powers smiled at Reverend Conners for the kind words spoken about his mother, Janice Powers. In fact, kind words were spoken by several people—many of whom he didn't know. There were so many things his mother did that he was unaware of, wonderful things, to help so many. He was proud to be her son.

How many days had he tried not to think of this day? How many days did he say to himself he would be strong; he would not cry—his mom would not want him to? Three years he'd told himself he needed to be prepared, but the moment the casket started to sink beneath the surface his strength betrayed him. As the casket sank, so did he—grief pushed him to his knees and covered him like a heavy cloak.

On his knees he watched his mother disappear into the depth of the hole. Ethan didn't know how long he stayed there; he simply knew that when he was finally able to look away from the grave, everyone was gone. He was glad; he had no desire to speak to anyone or put up a façade of strength. He'd used it all over the past three years.

Ethan's knees and back ached, but it didn't compare to the pain the empty space in his heart caused. His head also ached from the heavy perfume of the gardenias that permeated the air.

He needed to get back to his life in Bristol. Running his company from across the Atlantic was a difficult task, not to mention trying to oversee his airport in Australia, but he had refused to leave his mother's side. There was nothing keeping him in Albany anymore.

Standing, Ethan brushed the loose dirt from his knees, walked to one of the standing flower arrangements, picked a gardenia and smiled as he brought it to his nose. The heaviness of his grief fell away. He could see his mother so clearly in his mind. She had such great strength. She didn't complain and the only time he saw her cry was when she was happy for him. He placed the flower in his pocket.

Ethan closed his eyes and remembered how she'd taken him in, refusing to let him spend another night with his current foster parents. He'd cried when he thought they were going to send him back to them.

Ethan stiffened.

The grief-stricken muffled cries he heard were not from the memory of that day; they were real and nearby. Ethan looked around. He didn't see anyone then looked again, and nestled next to one of the well manicured graves was a small crumpled figure, crying.

Grief, as he knew first hand, is a very private and delicate matter. So what drew him towards the woman, he had no idea. Somehow he sensed her grief was too great to bear alone. Maybe it was the fact that his was so raw and new that he found himself standing over the woman then kneeling next to her. Not really knowing what to do nor wanting to startle her, he knelt beside her trying to offer his presence as a source of support. The woman's anguish was so great that the approach of a strange person did not cause her any alarm.

Ethan read the shiny black headstone.

Sparrow Ilarraza
You Were
Loved.

The date indicated Sparrow died two days before his or her first birthday. It was also the fifth anniversary of the baby's death. He figured the woman crying was the baby's mother.

Five years and her grief is still so strong?

How could such a tiny person carry so much pain and still be able to function?

The woman's wails halted and her breathing became erratic. Ethan realized she was hyperventilating. Without regard to him being a stranger, he reached for her.

"Shhh…you must calm down and breathe." He sat on his heels. Pain must have blinded her from fear and panic made her trusting. She reached for him and went into his arms willingly. "That's it." He rubbed her back to steady her breathing. "That's it…breathe."

Her crying subsided to only occasional hitches and still he held her. His cheek disappeared into the soft curls of her short black hair and like so many times since he found his mother lifeless in bed, he forgot about his own pain as he tried to absorb the woman's. Gently he held her as she trembled from the aftershocks of profound mourning.

Much too quickly she came to her senses and pulled away. She stood and Ethan watched the flowers printed around the bottom of her dark green dress switch back and forth as she quickly walked away without looking back.

He wondered who she was and if she would be ok. Did she mourn the baby this way each year? When he could no longer see her, he stood and walked to his car.

The wind blew softly as if it carried secrets long forgotten. Turning to look towards the fresh mound of new earth near the blue tent, Ethan added his own whispered secret before reaching for the door of the car. "I love you mother. I promise I will make everything right."

He closed his eyes, reached in his pocket and felt the flower, sighed and got into the car. Again, the woman came to mind. Even with a shroud of grief to mask her face, he'd seen her beauty.

Shifting the car into reverse, though faint, he could smell the soft scent of the woman's perfume mixed with the heavy fragrance of the flower in his pocket. She smelled good. Even her soft curly locks had smelled soft and womanly—like flowers. Ethan backed the car and drove away to prepare to get back to his life in England.

Two years later…
Boston

Chapter 1

Men Are Stupid

Sophia checked her watched again and waited for the students to take the stage. The school was an unscheduled stop in her busy schedule for the day, but she found herself always making time to visit the kids. They wanted her to see their dress rehearsal for the upcoming recital and she didn't have the heart to refuse.

Located in the inner city of Boston, Sophia was proud of Savage School of the Arts she'd helped start. It was a public school for students K-12 who were gifted artistically. Named after Augusta Savage—an African American teacher and sculptor who worked tirelessly for the equal rights of African Americans in the arts, the school's mission was to encourage minorities to experience more humanities than traditional schools offered. There was also an evening program for students whose school didn't offer any kind of art classes.

The foundation created by Joshua and Alexandra Phoenix was constantly raising money to offer schools grants so they would be able to offer various arts on their own campus. Savage School of the Arts had been in existence only since the beginning of the current school year, but there was already a waiting list for enrollment.

Sophia looked at her watch again and knew she would be pushing for time to meet Candice and Alexandra for their dress fitting. Candice Carwin was marrying Sophia's best friend, Landon Phoenix and had asked Sophia to be a bride's maid. Alexandra Phoenix was her matron of honor and also Candice's best friend and Landon's sister-in-law.

The idea of Landon getting married was still a bit unbelievable. She could just imagine women across Europe and the United States heavily veiled and in mourning over the loss of his bachelor-hood—not that he'd given any of them hope.

On the other hand, he'd fallen for Candice almost immediately, but pursuing her proved to be more difficult than he'd anticipated. She'd just gotten out of an abusive marriage and was in the process of being comfortable with her independence and not making other's insecurities affect her self-esteem.

Somehow Landon convinced her to let him join her on a trip through Europe, a birthday gift from Alex and Joshua. It was going to be his way of letting her get to know him better.

When Landon saved her from her ex-husband's clutches following a kidnapping in London, she realized all men were not like the man she'd married.

Sophia became good friends with the women when she was asked to help with the school arts fundraiser. Her expertise as a dance instructor and her involvement in movie chorography made her an ideal candidate for the benefit. Managing to get some of her A-list clients involved, the fundraiser turned out to be much more successful than anyone anticipated. So much so, an abandoned building was renovated and the school was established.

Lights danced across the floor of the large stage framed by heavy black velvet curtains, indicating they must be ready to start. The auditorium was the crown jewel of the school; it rivaled even the newly updated Crystal Theater in the art district.

She wondered how Landon and his partner Ethan were coming along with the revitalization of the art district. Their company Enrich Corp. bought several buildings in the area for the purpose of restoring them to their former glory.

Ms. Pakulski took the seat next to Sophia, grabbed and squeezed her hand in a silent plea for perfection. The tall thin ballet instructor with her thick Polish accent usually had more words than Sophia had time, but today her nervousness about the upcoming end of the year showcase was apparent.

"It's going to be ok, Helen." Sophia whispered.

Ms. Pakulski turned to her and smiled as the curtain closed and lights dimmed.

The curtains opened a short while later to an array of dragonfly wings glistening beneath the theater lights, giving the iridescence appearance of real wings. One dragonfly rose slowly and did a series of dances across the floor.

It was Bridgett.

Sophia's heart swelled in surprise.

She was one of the children whom she'd chosen to dance with her at the charity performance over a year ago. She was also one of the youngest and the shyest students of the bunch, but Sophia had seen her potential when she worked with the kids individually.

Back then, five year old Bridgett never smiled and only spoke when an adult asked her a question, but her dancing was so expressive, she didn't need words. The moment the music played the little girl became someone or something else. The notes from the music pushed and pulled, lifted and lowered and wove her into a new identity. Never had Sophia witnessed such a transformation in a child so young.

She'd told Sophia that she taught herself to dance. The girl's mother had been a ballet dancer who traveled often, dragging Bridgett on the road with her. When she became of school age, Child Protective Services intervened, saying she needed to be in school.

Her mother found work locally, rented a small apartment and enrolled Bridgett in school. However, one day her mom did not arrive to pick her up from school. All her things were still in the apartment, but no one knew what happened to Bridgett's mother.

She was placed in a foster home. Sophia checked on her often through Ms. Pakulski, though the dance teacher worried constantly that Bridgette would somehow get lost in the system.

Sophia watched her now and beamed with pride, hoping that somehow she'd had a hand in helping her come out of her shell.

Sophia turned to Ms. Pakulski with an awe-filled gaze. The older woman nodded with a knowing smile.

Look at her! She was taller now and still thin, but she looked healthy. Dancing was in her soul. Sophia watched as she tapped the wings of the other dragonflies. They slowly unfolded themselves and stood. The other girls were much older, at least ten, but Bridgett danced around them flawlessly.

Sophia was so caught up in the performance that she didn't notice the tears streaming down her face.

******

Seated at the bar of his favorite after work hangout, Ethan was oblivious to all the people around him. The game on the televisions positioned to be seen from every angle was reaching the top of the ninth inning. The Red Sox had such a lead; the pitcher would have to be wearing a blindfold to give up enough runs to lose the game. He'd stopped watching at the bottom of the seventh.

Ethan's cell phone rang. He looked at the screen; it was Landon.

"What's up Phoenix?"

"Candice and I are headed to Louisiana tonight. Will you be able to handle the Franklin deal without me?"

"Is everything ok? I thought we were all going together next Friday." Ethan wondered if he'd been so busy that he'd gotten the dates mixed up, but he was pretty sure he hadn't. "Besides, the Franklin deal is your baby. You've been trying to get old man Franklin's signature on that contract for the past five months."

"I know man, the timing stinks, but Candice's mom was brought into the hospital today. Her dad say's that the doctors think it may have been a stroke. I hate to drop this on you like this, but it can't be helped."

"Of course, I'll take care of it."

"Thanks, Ethan. Until we find out more, the wedding plans haven't changed. We all still plan to meet at Alex's place in Baton Rouge next week. But I don't want Candice going down there alone, especially since we don't know what's going on with her mom yet."

"I understand. Tell Jacob to fax over everything to my house tonight, so I can be as prepared as I know you are. Don't worry about things here. Go take care of your fiancé. Give her my best and keep us posted on her mom."

"Thanks again, man. I know this is going to blow your weekend, but—"

"Don't worry about it Landon;" Ethan interrupted, "I'll take care of everything while you're gone."

Seductive Pleasures

Landon disconnected the call and Ethan took a deep breath as he slid the phone back into his pocket. He knew all too well the hell Candice was probably going through. He hated hospitals. He'd spent too many nights there, worried sick about his mother.

Though he was genuinely concerned about Mrs. Carwin, Candice's mom, he couldn't help the sliver of a smile that touched his lips. Things couldn't have worked out better with the Franklin deal if he'd orchestrated it.

He knew Jacob, Landon's assistant, was probably faxing over all the documents at that very moment, but he was already more than prepared to go head to head with Bruce Franklin and his team of ethically challenged lawyers.

His partner, Landon Phoenix had controlling interest in their company, Enrich Corp., which was a stipulation Dixon Phoenix, Landon's father, insisted upon when he practically handed over the company to them.

Ethan and Landon had been all set to get investors to purchase a failing company called Global Green—both looking for a career change, but Dixon surprised them by gifting it to them when they found out he'd recently acquired Global Green as part of another takeover.

Seductive Pleasures

Landon, an airline pilot, had grown weary of contract renegotiations, union battles and waking up wondering what city he was in and what time of day it was. Wearing a watch only added to the confusion.

On the other hand, Ethan owned a small airport in Australia, but during the year after his mother died, he was earnestly researching companies to invest in and run while living in England. He was tired of living and working from two different continents and was plagued with the constant barrage of security changes and regulations from the ICAO. The International Civil Aviation Organization and IATA (International Air Transport Association) were a staple in Ethan's daily conversations.

It had become too difficult to enjoy his love of air travel while running an airport; even though he didn't have to deal with many commercial airlines, aviation law was taking all the fun out of running the airport.

He was ready to put his business expertise towards an adventure that would be meaningful and wouldn't slowly tear the soul from his love of flying.

Coincidently, meeting Landon Phoenix at an air safety conference was the catalyst that would change his life. Ethan's lack of controlling interest would soon prove to be beneficial. Bruce Franklin was just another step in putting his plans in motion.

"It won't work, ya know."

As if privy to his private thoughts, the voice echoed a fear that he refused to entertain. As Ethan curiously turned towards the voice laced with the dialect that personified local Bostonian lower and middle class, he felt a nudge on his bar stool. He looked down to find a pair of leopard print stilettos resting on his foot rail.

Ethan's eyes climbed the trail of shapely legs that seemed to go on forever and much too exposed for the fifty degree spring weather.

The gold fringes on the hem of the dress reminded him of a gaudy pillow he used to play with at his grandmother's house. He'd pretended it was a magic carpet.

When his gaze finally made it to her face, he found much too much eye make-up and the overtly red lipstick was reminiscent of those grotesque clowns that most little children are afraid of. She was no magic carpet ride—not one he wanted to take, anyway.

She smiled, making her mouth appear even more repugnant. Clearly getting the wrong impression of his slow thorough appraisal of her, she leaned in closer. He wondered briefly if his face communicated his thoughts and decided he didn't really care.

"It won't work, ya know." She said again.

"What won't work?" Ethan asked, more with his facial expression than his words.

The woman leaned towards him and whispered, "The stern look on your face." She smiled and Ethan lifted a brow. "You use it as a shield to keep people from disturbing you." She sat up proudly as if she'd just revealed the meaning of life.

Ethan laid a bill next to his bottle of beer and signaled the bartender before he turned towards the woman. He leaned in towards her and whispered, "I need to work on my methods." then stood and walked away.

He should've left the bar and gone home, but found himself taking the stairs to the Tailgate Lounge. It was a casual restaurant upstairs that sometimes hosted a live band. He wasn't looking for companionship, at least not tonight. He just didn't feel like going to an empty house. He'd dated a few women since he moved to Boston; however none of them sparked his interest enough to want to see again. Especially, not since Jessie Stevens tried to trap him into getting her pregnant.

Ethan shook his head trying to rid the memory from his mind. She was the last person he wanted to think about. It wasn't that he didn't want a relationship; he just hadn't met anyone worth the effort. It also didn't help that he was haunted by a woman in his dreams.

The moment he stepped off of the elevator, he saw her. He had no idea she was in town. He'd yet to see a woman to pull off that short curly hair cut like she did. It was black as a raven's belly and he dreamt about the way it would feel against his cheek as he nuzzled into it.

Everything she wore seemed to be designed just for her small frame. She had on a short charcoal gray dress with gray leggings, belted at the waist. Her black suede boots covered her legs nearly to the thigh. The outfit was ultra-sexy without revealing any of her golden skin.

Sophia was dancing effortlessly to a salsa tune. She was in her element—sexy without being provocative. Ethan sat at a table, eyes on her. He had to admit, she was breathtaking and envied the guy who seemed to place his hands a bit too low on her back and hold her a little too close to be a casual acquaintance.

Seductive Pleasures

Ethan had no idea how either of the two moved their feet so fast, spun around constantly and kept up with the beat. Sophia twirled around and intimately traveled her hands across the guy's shoulder. He felt the tiny stab of envy.

He knew that was the nature of the dance, but couldn't help wondering if Sophia was there with the guy and then wondered why he even cared. She smiled seductively and seemed to melt into her dance partner.

At the end of the dance, Sophia slid down his leg into a split. Everyone else had long since stopped dancing just to watch the two of them and when she ended in the split, the crowd exploded in applause.

Although he'd seen Sophia dance before, he'd never seen her so...so fluid and provocative. Before, it was a practiced routine or just a casual dance with Landon or his brother Joshua.

Ethan found himself clapping and whistling along with the rest of the crowd and again wondered what she was doing in town. Landon was her best friend and he knew she was part of the wedding party as was he, but the wedding party weren't meeting in Louisiana until a few days before the wedding.

The band immediately began another song and those who'd stopped, started dancing again while some of the spectators headed for the dance floor. From the reaction of the crowd, it was a popular song.

Ethan's eyes found Sophia again. She was still on the floor with the same guy. He seemed to be trying to talk her into another dance and she was unsuccessfully trying to remove his hand from around her waist. The guy twirled her around and she stumbled a bit.

The man pulled her much to close, lifted her thigh to his waist and took the liberty of letting his hand explore the length of it down to the top of her boot. Again, Ethan saw Sophia attempt without success to push the guy away.

He hesitated at first since he knew for certain that she didn't care for him much, mostly because he went out of his way to avoid her. Sophia was a distraction he couldn't afford. His attraction for her was much too dangerous for his future plans.

He didn't want to make a scene, especially since she was convinced that he hated her, but he couldn't sit back and watch while that bastard practically molested her on the dance floor. On his feet and headed towards her, he braced himself—not from him, from her.

The moment he walked up to Sophia, he knew she was drunk. His dark eyes captured hers.

"There you are Sweetheart; I've been waiting for you downstairs. Are you ready?" Ethan smiled down at Sophia before directing a pointed stare at the man holding on to her.

"Excuse us."

The two words were barbed with an unspoken challenge.

"The lady seems to be having a good time." The man replied.

Ethan's smile did not reach his eyes and his anger was held in check because he could tell Sophia was barely able to hold herself up.

"For some reason you take for granted my words indicated you had an option."

The smile never left his face as he took a step closer to the man. Ethan firmly grabbed the man's wrist still draped around Sophia's waist and bent it at an awkward but obviously painful angle.

"I said, 'Excuse us.'"

The man released Sophia immediately, grabbed his wrist with is other hand and watched Ethan walk with her to a table to get her purse and then to the elevator.

Inside the elevator, Ethan turned to Sophia.

"Are you ok?" He asked.

"Are *you* ok?" She flung back as she stepped towards him. The elevator moved abruptly causing her to lose her balance and fall into his chest. She looked up at him. "You're not afraid of being this close to me?"

Her eyes closed a bit and she smiled, before looking at him again. "I mean, aren't you afraid I may turn you into stone or something?"

Ethan didn't move her away. He simply looked down at her and held her gingerly at her side in case she stumbled again.

"I'll take my chances."

"Men are stupid."

He cocked an eyebrow at her.

"Is that right?"

"Yes, and you are the stupidest of the stupid men." She slurred.

"Why is that?" Why in the hell was it taking so long for the elevator to go two floors?

"Because you're afraid of girls." She started to laugh.

The elevator doors opened and Ethan hoped she would be able to walk out with him without anyone knowing how drunk she was. How much did she have to drink?

Ethan placed his arm around Sophia's waist. "Come on Sophia; let me get you out of here. You're drunk."

Stating the obvious was not a smart move.

She pulled away from him, too quickly. She staggered a bit. He looked around, but no one was paying attention.

"I'm not going anywhere with you." She opened her purse and dug around in it, mumbling something in Spanish.

In English she said. "I'm not going anywhere with the stupidest man in town who is afraid of girls." She pulled out a key and walked towards him.

"Men. Are. Stupid." She punctuated each word with a finger in his chest.

"Yes we are, but there is no way I'm letting you drive." He stood there with his hands in his pocket taking her abuse and thought, "Who gets drunk on a Wednesday night?"

Sophia had no response to his admission. He figured he needed to say something else clever enough to get her to leave with him.

"How about you ride with me and tell me how stupid men are."

She frowned, letting the idea roll around in her head.

"Ok, but it may take a while." She snapped her purse closed.

Ethan couldn't help the chuckle that escaped his lips. He was glad she was so agreeable.

"Ok Sophia. It's a deal."

Chapter 2

Have We Met?

The sliver of daylight that invaded the room seemed to split Sophia's head in half. She pulled the bed covering over her head and tried to lie as still as humanly possible. Sleep claimed her again.

She was stuck inside an elephant's belly. The heart was nearby because the beating of it was nearly deafening. It was difficult to move and she couldn't scream because someone stuffed cotton in her mouth. Between the heartbeat intervals she heard the light fluttering sounds of piano keys. If only she could see. She squeezed through the huge organs of the elephant, groping for freedom.

Through the fog of the dream, Sophia remembered the covers were over her head. She pulled them down, this time, relieved that she was no longer in the dark. She still couldn't speak and the elephant's heart beat louder, yet the piano sounds were no longer heard. Disappointment settled in, because she was sure the music was the secret to getting out of the elephant.

In the distance, Sophia heard the sultry sounds of Santana's "Maria Maria." It was her ring tone. She turned toward the music, still not quite awake. Her head violently protested to the sudden motion. She lay still again, bringing her arm to cover her eyes from the light. A low groan was trapped behind her closed lips. She figured if she could just lie still she would be fine.

Although her eyes were closed, after a while Sophia was awake and fully aware of the dreadful hangover. Her mouth was dry, but any kind of water source, she figured, was too far away to do anything about it. She would just have to lie still and wait for death to find her.

Sophia remembered her cell phone rang what seemed like hours before, but was probably only a few minutes. Not yet brave enough to move again, she thought she would attempt to at least open her eyes.

With great effort she moved her arm and willed her eyes to open. The light. Oh God. It was nearly blinding and the small effort made her nauseous.

Dear God please don't let me throw up. The words became a mantra that was repeated over and over.

She willed the bout of nausea to pass.

Why oh why did she drink so much? A low groan rattled her lips.

She remembered.

Two words—Ethan Powers.

Seductive Pleasures

She'd seen him the moment she walked into Cliques. Whenever she was in town she made it a point to visit the sports bar Alex owned; she enjoyed the atmosphere and live music in the establishment.

She was supposed to meet Candice and Alex at the bar after their final dress fitting but Candice received news that her mom was ill while they were still at the bridal shop and she and Alex were making arrangements to fly to Baton Rouge along with Joshua and Landon.

She'd decided to go to Cliques anyway. It pissed her off just being in the same place as Ethan, because it was so frustrating not to know why he treated her with such distain. The confusing part was he was totally different when they first met.

The first time she'd met Ethan was when she was asked to help with the group of underprivileged children who wanted to take dance lessons. It was difficult for her to leave her dance studio in New York, but she couldn't turn down the opportunity to be a part of raising money so kids could be involved in the arts. So she put one of the other instructors, Kristina, in charge for the rest of the summer, in order to prepare for the fall fundraiser.

Seductive Pleasures

She dropped everything and flew to Boston for one of the planning meetings. In fact, the meeting had taken place in the sports bar where she now found herself frequenting whenever she was in town.

Ethan and Sophia met in the parking lot of Cliques when she accidently dinged his car door with hers. The moment he emerged from his vehicle, he stood and just stared at her. With haunting eyes, he looked at her as if he'd seen a ghost.

"I'm so sorry. The wind pulled the door right out of my hand." She said, trying to ignore his concentrated appraisal of her.

He looked at her so intently she began to wonder if he was someone she should know.

"Have we met?"

She appraised *him*. Surely she would have remembered such enigmatic dark eyes, though she couldn't shake the fact that he looked vaguely familiar. His skin was light like hers, but he had an exotic look about him—a mixture of African American ancestry and some other ethnicity, she was sure. It was his thick brows and black curly hair that gave him a Middle Eastern look. He also stood tall with an air of confidence that she liked. She liked it a lot.

Seductive Pleasures

Her attraction was immediate and she figured many women fell prey to his dreamy dark eyes and mysterious air.

He never answered her question. Instead, he'd given her a welcoming smile and told her the car was just a rental. He didn't seem to care less about the car, but she offered to buy him a drink anyway. She thought she owed him at least that much for not making a fuss over the car.

It wasn't so much as she felt she needed a peace offering of sorts, for some reason she wanted to get to know him. Well, not for *some* reason. She thought that if she had to be in Boston away from her work, she may as well make it worth her while.

He was handsome, yes, but more than that, he was sexy as sin and just from the brief encounter in the parking lot, he seemed friendly. He put her at ease immediately. They discovered both were there to meet someone who hadn't arrived yet.

Sophia and Ethan walked in the doors of the upscale sports bar, looked around not seeing either of their parties. They sat at the bar and ordered the drink she'd offered.

"I notice you have an accent. Is it rude of me to ask where you're from?" He asked.

"Why would that be rude?"

"I don't know, but some people take offence when asked, especially if they grew up all their lives in the states."

"I'm not offended in the least." She picked up her drink, placed it on the bar again and licked the corner of her mouth, totally unaware of the affect her gesture had on him. "I'm from a small city in South America called Maracay."

"Ah...Venezuela."

"Si, do you know it?"

"I know of it. A few baseball players from there traveled to Australia often and used my small airport in Brisbane when they traveled. I'm a huge baseball fan. There are a lot of great ball players from Maracay."

"Australia?" She cocked her head to the side. "You sound more like you're from upstate New York than down under."

Ethan smiled, impressed that she'd picked up his dialect so easily.

"I grew up in Albany, but just recently moved to Boston after dividing my time between Brisbane and London."

"Wow, that's a big divide. What could possibly have you straddling the equator like that?"

"It's a long story. Maybe I'll tell you over breakfast one morning."

Sophia raised a brow.

"I'll hold you to that."

The conversation flowed easily. They laughed out loud causing several heads to turn to look at them.

Ethan found Sophia to be even more intriguing than he originally thought and found himself wanting to know more about her.

"Tell me all about Sophia."

She smiled and held his eyes with hers. Their gaze was so intense, she had to look away. She could have sworn that he'd taken a peak underneath the skirt of her soul. She took a cleansing breath and let her finger trace the rim of her glass.

"Be careful what you ask for, Señor Ethan Powers."

Ethan loved the way his name rolled off her tongue. When she said his first name she pronounced each syllable crisp and clear. He loved her accent. It made him just want to sit and listen to her talk for hours.

"I know exactly what I'm asking for."

A curious brow rose slowly on her forehead as she wondered if he really did. She figured she would give him the customary facts.

"Well, you know where I'm from." She smiled. "I currently live in New York City where I teach all forms of Latin dance to adults… That's about it."

Ethan placed his elbow on the bar and rested his head in his hand as he drank in the sight of her.

"What makes you laugh? What excites you?" He traced a line from her wrist to a knuckle. "What makes you sad?" The last question brushed over her with such sincerity it made her ache.

She studied him for the longest time and for a moment he didn't think she would answer him.

"The present."

"Present?"

"You know, what's happening right now." She said with a soft chuckle. "Here, talking with you makes me laugh."

He lifted his chin towards her and asked in a tone meant only for her. "What excites you?"

"My fantasies." The simple admission landed between them almost as an unspoken challenge or subtle request.

Ethan raised a brow, but didn't ask her to elaborate.

"And what makes you sad."

She turned her eyes towards the mirror behind the bar and whether she was looking at her reflection or not, he couldn't tell. Ethan didn't realize he was holding his breath until she spoke.

"My past."

Ethan leaned in until his mouth was next to her ear.

"How does the future make you feel?"

She turned her head to look at him and grabbed her bottom lip with her teeth.

"Exhausted."

He wanted her.

Right now. His need pressed against the zipper of his slacks as physical evidence that if he didn't change the subject right now and turn his mind to something else, he would be dragging her out of Cliques like a caveman claiming his woman.

He blinked slowly inhaling deeply.

"So you're a dancer?"

Her smile told him she was quite aware of what he was doing and completely understood why.

"Yes. An instructor and choreographer mostly, but I still perform on occasion."

"What kind of dancing do you do?"

"A real dancer can dance to fit the music." She crossed her legs, showing off her golden calves and toned thighs and gave him a slow crooked smile. "My body has a mind of its own; it just moves to the music."

He gave her a crooked grin. "I sing and play the piano." He leaned closer to her ear. "That's music, right?"

Sophia put her lips next to his ear and whispered, "The best kind."

She remembered feeling their intense sexual attraction and longed to explore it.

"To be continued." He whispered back. Ethan sat up. "My business partner is here, but here is my ca—" He'd reached into the pocket of his sports coat at the same time she heard Landon call her name.

"Soph! You made it!"

Just as she was about to shoot Landon a dirty look for interrupting her conversation, he scooped her off the stool and spun her around.

"I haven't seen you in forever!" Landon said as he squeezed her tightly. "It seems as though since I've moved back to the states, I've talked to you even less than when I lived in London."

Sophia didn't remember much after that, but she felt an instant coolness once Ethan found out she and Landon were friends. Landon, nor anyone else who arrived later, noticed. Of course they had not been privy to the conversation she and Ethan had only moments before, but others should have noticed how aloof he was with her. And she was never able to speak to Ethan privately again that night.

The change in Ethan left Sophia wondering if she'd actually been talking to the same guy before Landon showed up.

She'd been thinking about Ethan while she sat in Cliques and decided to drink to clear her head of him.

"Clearly not smart." She mumbled.

What happened last night? How did she get back to the hotel? Obviously she hadn't wound up dead in a ditch somewhere, though that idea sounded a tad more welcoming than the pain that roared through her head.

Sophia slowly turned over onto her stomach, waited for the nausea to fade and snuggled into the pillow, giving up on getting out of bed for the moment. Sleep found her quickly.

She looked around and watched the pigs move quickly to barricade the door. She couldn't hear what they were saying and found that when she tried to ask them to speak up, she couldn't talk. The bed was really comfortable so she didn't try to get up to help them, just watched as they used the straw, bricks and sticks

41

to brace the door. There was a knock on the door and the pigs hid in the closet. Again, Sophia tried to ask them what was happening but she could only make soft mewing sounds like a cat. She saw the door opening and a large wolf standing there with a case of Popsicles. He walked over to her and wiped her face with one of the popsicles and stroked her hair. The wolf, too, was whispering like the pigs had, but she thought she heard him say,

"Why are you so beautiful? Why can't I get you out of my mind? Why am I seduced by the mere fact that I can't have you?"

"Do you have an orange one?" She managed to voice in spite of her tongue, thick and dry like caked mud. She rolled onto her side so the wolf could reach her forehead. The coolness was helping.

"An orange what?" Ethan asked as he placed the towel on the nightstand.

"Popsicle." Sophia answered still clinging to the dream.

"Do they normally help you with a hangover?" She stiffened.

Coherent enough to know that movement meant pain, she slowly willed her eyes to open. A wall and blue sheets were the only things in view.

Neither of which she recognized.

42

She looked around wildly without moving her head, not wanting to risk stirring the pain waiting to assault her body.

Where was she?

She was sure it was not her hotel room. Suddenly, panic held her immobile as she remembered the threatening letter she'd received before she left Manhattan. The letter said she'd be sorry and vengeance would come soon.

She tried to find clarity in her fog-dense mind to remember the last thing she'd done.

The dance floor!

She remembered dancing with a guy who she'd flirted with at first but later brushed off when he'd become too aggressive. She'd only agreed to dance with him not to cause a scene and found he was a very good dancer. Though, the last thing she remembered was telling him to let her go.

Dear Lord, did she go home with him? She didn't feel naked, but...

Sophia's heart beat fast and her chest heaved up and down. She could feel the weight of someone sitting on the bed. Too afraid to find out who it was she had yet to turn.

One, because the nausea was building again and two, she was afraid to face the consequences of her overindulgence of alcohol.

"It's ok, Sophia. It's me, Ethan." He said it as if he'd known what she was thinking.

Ethan?

What was she doing with Ethan?

She relaxed… slightly.

Sophia rolled over, focused her eyes as best as she could and there he was.

Ethan Powers.

She closed her eyes, relieved it was not the guy from the bar or worse.

"The wolf… Of course." She muttered.

"Excuse me?"

"Where am I and what am I doing with you?" she asked flatly.

"You were drunk. You couldn't drive and you passed out in the middle of you telling me how stupid my species is—well… me especially."

He smiled at her. Something she hadn't seen directed towards her since the first night they met—before he found out she and Landon were best friends. She didn't want to think about that night right now or the intense attraction she had for him...still.

"And so you just brought me home with you?" Her displeasure apparent.

"What would you have me do with you? I don't know where you're staying."

"You could've just left me in my car."

She wondered if her breath smelled as foul as it tasted.

"And risk you driving drunk? No ma'am."

Sophia didn't want to admit it, but she liked the feeling of him sitting next to her on the bed. It was comforting to know he was concerned about her.

Ethan looked down at her with that crooked smile that she hated to adore, but did anyway—looking all fresh and clean-shaven. Smelling like sex dipped in sin, which is a heavenly intoxicating, panty-dropping-making-a-woman-stupid, aroma.

In turn, she reeked of leftover vodka laced with hangover morning breath and imminent queasiness.

"You could've put me in a cab." She closed her eyes and brought her arm across her face again.

"And what if you would've passed out in the cab? God knows what would've happened to you." He shook his head. "My mom didn't raise me like that."

Sophia moved her arm and looked up at Ethan. There was something different in his voice.

Seductive Pleasures

"Thank you, Ethan." She said softly. Sophia began to sit up, slapped her hand over her mouth and looked around the room frantically.

Ethan moved off the bed quickly and pointed towards a door across the room. She had no time to ask questions, jumped out of the bed and made it to the bathroom just in time to "pay homage to the porcelain god," as many people so aptly called throwing up after drinking far far too much.

Never in her life had she experienced such humiliation. She wasn't much of a drinker and wondered how people could drink to such excess if this was the impending result.

Sophia was in the bathroom so long, Ethan knocked on the door to check on her. "I'm ok, she managed to squeak before another wave of vomiting brought her closer to death, because surely one could not recover from such violent uprising from their insides.

Just when she thought she was completely emptied out, she wearily lunged towards the toilet again. She opened her eyes as she reached for the handle to flush away the remnants of a night she would never repeat and noticed the blood on the toilet handle and seat.

Seductive Pleasures

It was the last thing she saw as she slid onto the cold tile. She couldn't tell if the thumping she heard was from the door, her head or the elephant's heartbeat.

Chapter 3

Just a Precaution

He figured she was probably embarrassed. Throwing up on the other side of the door from a guy whom she thought disliked her, was probably not on her top-ten list of things to do. Ethan decided not to bother her and let nature run its course. He'd had a typical college experience; he knew the results of too much drinking, all too well. He was nearly forty-one now and never indulged to excess anymore.

When several minutes of silence passed he began to worry.

"Sophia…Sophia, are you ok?"

No response.

Embarrassed or not, he was going in there. A cool towel to wipe her mouth or rest on her head would be welcomed, even if she thought he was a wolf.

Ethan was in no way prepared for the scene he walked in on. The hair stood on his arms and his heart slammed against his chest. His hands trembled. He remembered finding his mother just like this one morning. It was the day he learned she had cancer.

He took the scene in quickly. There was blood on the front of her camisole, her hand and the toilet.

48

This was not hangover sickness. This was something else.

Something dangerous and deadly.

Ethan lived about two miles from the hospital. He didn't want to wait for an ambulance; instead, he scooped Sophia into his arms, grabbed her purse off the dresser and headed out the door.

It only took a few moments to drive to the hospital. She was breathing, but unconscious. Ethan told the doctors she'd drunk too much last night and woke up with a terrible hangover and vomiting.

They asked him if it was possible that someone could have slipped something into her drink. He immediately thought of the guy at the bar, but was not sure. Then they asked if there was a possibility that she was pregnant.

Pregnant?

His gut twisted.

Could she be pregnant? He thought a moment and figured there was a slim chance because she'd been drinking. Though, of course she was a woman of childbearing age, but just the thought of her creating a baby with someone left him…empty.

"Sir, is there a chance she could be pregnant?"

"I…I'm not sure." He finally uttered.

They'd taken her back nearly an hour ago. The nurse assured him that they would let him know something as soon as they had any information. He filled out the hospital forms as best as he could and gave them her insurance card from her wallet, but there was very little that he knew about Sophia.

Why hadn't he known her last name?

He knew why. It was because he went out of his way to know as little as he could about her.

Sophia Ilarraza. Thirty-six years old, lives in Manhattan, New York, 5'3", brown eyes, black hair and is an organ donor—information he received from her driver's license. The purse contained her wallet, lip gloss, hotel card, a rental car key and a small compact that held face powder and a mirror.

Why hadn't he grabbed her cell phone?

Ethan had no idea what she was allergic to, if anything, her blood type or if she'd eaten dinner—all the things the nurse asked him when he brought her in. He'd told them she was his fiancée, but for all he knew, they were withholding information from him until the cops came to arrest him.

Ethan wondered if he should call Landon, but decided to wait until he had more information. He looked around at the peach walls of the waiting room that matched the cushions of the seats. He was glad there were several seats and the emergency room was not crowded so he wouldn't have to sit near anyone and they feel compelled to talk to him.

He really wished he knew more about Sophia at that moment. Did she have family? Friends? The only people he'd seen her with were Landon, Landon's sister-in-law Alexandra and Landon's fiancée, Candice.

Ethan pulled the driver's license from her purse again and looked at the picture. Her hair was longer and surprisingly straight. Her eyes bore into him, demanding secrets. He was sure as a kid they yielded her anything her heart desired.

"Sir, are you the gentleman who brought in Ms. Ilarraza?"

Ethan immediately stood. He hated talking to doctors. They always seemed to bring such bad news.

The doctor looked weary and unconcerned.

"You are her…" He paused as if he was hoping Ethan would fill in the blank. It was clearly too much trouble to have a patient with no family present. Time would need to be taken to contact the next of kin.

"Her fiancée, Ethan Powers." He filled in. "How is she?"

The doctor looked as if he'd had a long shift and was ready to get home, which worried Ethan.

"I'm Dr. Patel, Mr. Powers. Your fiancé is going to be fine after several days of rest. We are going to keep her overnight just as a precaution. She will be restricted to clear liquids for a couple of days but after that she should be able to begin to take on small doses of food."

"As a precaution for what? Did she have alcohol poisoning? She drank quite a bit last night."

"Has Ms. Ilarraza recently traveled to the Mediterranean?"

Of course Ethan had no idea and wondered what that had to do with her current condition. There was no passport in her purse. He decided to be honest with the doctor.

"If she has, it was without my knowledge. I'm pretty sure she has not. Why? What does being in the Mediterranean have anything to do with her vomiting blood?"

Ethan was instantly confused. He heard a baby wailing and wished he could just leave and take Sophia home with him.

The doctor seemed to be annoyed by the question.

"Ms. Ilarraza came in with white chameleon poisoning. Traces of the plant's toxins were found in her blood stream. One of the symptoms of the poison is vomiting blood. There was no food in her stomach which most likely is the cause of the excessive hangover symptoms and why she was affected by it so acutely." The doctor pulled off his glasses, wiped them with the hem of his coat and put them back on. "The nurse will tell you what room your fiancé is in, Mr. Powers."

The doctor turned to walk away as if he had just told Ethan, Sophia had a stomach virus.

"I'm sorry Dr. Patel, I know you're probably at the end of your shift and you're tired, but I'm going to need a bit more information about this." Ethan frowned and stared down at the man who pulled his glasses off again. "What is white chameleon poisoning? Should I call the police? Did someone deliberately poison her?"

The doctor sighed and put his glasses back on, looked up at Ethan and offered a practiced look of concern. "Sir, we have lots of patients waiting to be seen. It could have been as simple as her eating a salad and thinking the thistle was an artichoke."

"With all due respect doctor, I don't give a damn about your other patients. My concern is with the patient I brought in here, *unconscious*." Ethan leaned a little closer to the doctor without trying to appear threatening. The doctor raised more questions than gave answers. "Now, are you going to take the time to explain to me what's going on or do I have to speak to someone else?"

And as if fate intervened, Dixon Phoenix walked in. Landon and Joshua's father and his wife were major contributors to St. Francis Medical Center. In fact, they sponsored an entire children's wing.

Dixon spotted Ethan right away.

"Ethan, my boy, what brings you to the emergency room?" Before Ethan could get a word out Dixon asked, "There isn't anything wrong is there?"

"Actually Mr. *Phoenix*…" Ethan's eyes rested on the doctor when he said "Phoenix." Dr. Patel's eyes grew wide at the mention of Dixon's last name. Ethan looked at Dixon again, "It's Sophia." He turned back to the doctor. "It appears that the good doctor here has too many patients to properly advise me on her condition."

"*Our* Sophia? She's in town?" Dixon had grown quite fond of Sophia over the past year and was terribly concerned to hear she was in the hospital.

"Yes. Sir." Ethan wanted to be smug but was far too concerned about Sophia being poisoned.

"What's your name?" Dixon asked the doctor.

54

"I am Dr. Raj Patel." The doctor responded wiping his glasses again.

"What's going on with Sophie?"

"I'm only at liberty to give information to her relatives and since Mr. Powers is her fiancé and was the one who brought her in…" Dixon lifted an eyebrow at Ethan. Ethan pretended not to notice.

The doctor continued, "I felt it was within his right to receive the information." Before the doctor could protest further, Ethan interrupted.

"Dixon, she was unconscious when I brought her in and Dr. Patel says she was poisoned."

"Poisoned!" Dixon exclaimed. A few people began to take an interest in their conversation.

Dixon looked at Dr. Patel pointedly waiting for confirmation.

The doctor gave a annoyed sigh before he spoke. "Ms. Ilarraza had traces of white chameleon poison in her blood stream."

"And you see no need for concern?"

"She is resting fine and will regain her strength very quickly. She simply needs a few days of rest.

Dixon refused to hear anything further from the man. "Dr. Patel, you may see to your other patients. I've heard enough. Ms. Ilarraza needn't concern you any longer. I will get Dr. Vecell to take over the case."

"Sir, you don't have the authority to—"

Dixon was already pulling out his cell phone.

"Do you want to try me and see?"

Dixon rarely used his money to bulldoze people, but he felt the situation warranted it. Sophia was his son's best friend.

Indignant, Dr. Patel walked away; his movements stiff and awkward. Both men watched him storm off wiping his glasses.

Dixon spoke first, "Go and make sure our girl is ok. I'll get in touch with Dr. Vecell right away. I know he's in the hospital now; we're supposed to play golf after he checked on a few patients this morning. He'll give us the answers we need."

"Thank you, Dixon. I have a feeling something isn't quite right with this poisoning business." Ethan reached out a hand to Dixon. Dixon shook it and patted Ethan on his shoulder.

"Uh...If you don't mind, Sir, can you keep this just between the two of us right now? I don't know how Sophia will feel about anyone knowing about her being here."

"Sure thing, Son."

Ethan wasn't so sure how Sophia would feel about him being there at all but he was hell bent on finding out what was going on with her.

Chapter 4

Missing Gloria

"Gloria Davis, if you needed time off from work, all you had to do was say so."

The woman opened her eyes slowly and smiled. He felt like it had been months instead of only a couple of days since he saw those eyes of hers that always reminded him of sparkling jewels—mysterious green with flecks of hazel. He never tired of looking at them.

"Mr. Phoenix. You didn't have to come up here." Her voice was tired and he watched her eyes close again. "Trina has access to everything." Gloria peeked up at Dixon and frowned. "Is anything wrong?"

Dixon walked up to the hospital bed and placed her hand in his.

"How many times do I have to tell you to call me Dixon?" He smiled at her. "For God sakes woman, you know me better than anyone." The pad of his thumb slowly stroked the back of her hand. "The only thing wrong at work is you're not there." His voice trailed off to nearly a whisper as he looked at her hand in his. "And I don't mean, just because you're great at your job."

Dixon's eyes met Gloria's and he moved a twist of her hair from her forehead with his free hand. She wore it naturally in coiled locks that he always felt gave her such a regal air. "I miss my friend, Gloria. I miss *you*." He caressed the side of her face and she pressed her cheek into his hand.

"Who told you I was in the hospital?"

"It doesn't matter who told me, the question is, why didn't *you* tell me? Why go through all the trouble of making me think you were on vacation?"

"It's just such a private matter Mr.—" He lifted his chin in protest. "Dixon."

Dixon's voice was soft and apologetic when he spoke. "I'm sorry for intruding, but I had to see for myself that you were ok."

Gloria's eyes closed and after a few moments, Dixon thought she'd dozed.

"I'll be fine in a few days Dixon. They're letting me go tomorrow." She opened her eyes, looked at him and smiled. "What have you been eating for lunch?"

An easy smile played at the corners of his mouth. "You know good and well what I've been eating for lunch, woman."

Gloria always made sure he had a healthy lunch, though it was when he'd found out she'd been switching his carrot cake from his favorite deli with one that she'd baked herself, that he knew the extent of her efforts. She started making a sugar-free version of the cake because he'd mentioned to her that his doctor wanted him to cut back on his sugar intake. He couldn't remember his wife, Jocelyn, ever baking anything for him or even caring if he ate at all.

Since Gloria was out of the office, her assistant Trina made sure he had his lunch when he decided to stay in the office and work through lunch. He didn't know how Gloria pulled it off but the carrot cake arrived even without her.

"So Trina followed orders for once?" Gloria tried to reposition herself and winced.

Dixon's smile faded and was replaced by a genuine frown of concern. He was far more worried about the woman than what he had for lunch.

"Are you sure you'll be ready to leave tomorrow?"

"Yes, I'm ready to leave now. They don't let you rest in the hospital. Every hour or so, there's someone coming in to poke, prod or check something." She looked up at him. "I'm ready to go home."

"You can barely move without wincing. How in the world are you ready to go home?" Dixon walked over to the flowers near the window before she could answer. He knew it was none of his business, but decided to ask anyway. "Who's picking you up?"

Dixon noticed several arrangements, one he'd hand-picked and had delivered. It was the largest of the assortment. He wondered why others knew she was in the hospital and he had not.

When he turned towards her again, he found she really had dozed this time. He smiled and walked over to the hospital bed. At that time, a nurse walked in saying she needed to check Gloria's vitals.

Gloria opened her eyes, "See."

Dixon smiled and nodded his head, understanding why she wanted to go home.

"What are you doing here anyway? Aren't you supposed to be in Concord with Mrs. Phoenix?" She tried to sit up, winced and eased back on the pillow. "I hate this." She hissed.

"Hate what?"

"Being incapacitated." She closed her eyes and took a few deep breaths.

"Just keep still and rest so you will be back to yourself quickly." Dixon watched the nurse take Gloria's blood pressure.

"Didn't you see your flight reservations on the desk?" She asked.

Dixon frowned and looked at Gloria, confused by her question.

"Flight reservations?"

"Yes, you're supposed to be at the capital for Rep. Todd Cloudy's fundraiser events."

"Cloudy doesn't give a damn if I'm there or not, he just wants my check!"

The nurse glanced at Dixon and quickly finished writing Gloria's information on the chart then left them alone again.

"And Jocelyn was ok with that?" Gloria asked.

Dixon's jaw tensed and he took a deep breath.

"I'm sorry Mr. Phoenix. I didn't mean to pry. I was just wondering why you were here instead of with your wife in Concord."

"No, *I'm* sorry." Dixon rubbed his forehead and walked towards the flowers again. He touched the petals of a yellow rose surrounded by a mixture of flowers he couldn't name. "I just get so frustrated thinking about what Jocelyn is 'ok' with?"

"I'm sorry; I really didn't mean anything by it. I just wanted to know if Trina had forgotten to give you your itinerary."

He shook his head.

"No, no, my dear. You have nothing to be sorry about." After a long heavy sigh, he continued. "I'm frustrated with myself. How in the hell did I end up so unhappy?"

Gloria didn't say a word. She simply looked at him and wondered if he would continue.

"It's like I've been asleep for nearly forty years and I've just woke up, but everything has changed. Everything is different and I don't recognize… even myself."

Dixon looked out the window and watched a flock of birds land in a tree near the parking lot.

"My sons both seemed to have survived my slumber, but I nearly lost Landon." He watched the birds swoop in and out of the tree, oblivious of the people moving around beneath it. "Joshua and Landon have moved on. They have great women by their sides and I'm envious as hell." Dixon took a deep breath still looking out the window. "You asked why I was here instead of with my wife in Concord?" He hesitated. "I'm here because there is no other place I'd rather be."

Dixon paused another moment before he turned to look at Gloria, afraid he'd exposed too much of himself. He walked to the bed and found she was fast asleep. He smiled, placed her hand in his as he'd done when he greeted her, and squeezed it gently. He leaned over to place a tender kiss on her forehead.

Managing no more than a hoarse whisper, he said, "You woke me up."

Gently squeezing Gloria's hand again, Dixon turned and walked out of the room.

Gloria opened her eyes, softly touched her forehead with the tips of her fingers and with a feather-like touch, placed them on her lips. Her long sigh filled the room—an apt companion to her wistful, misty eyes.

Chapter 5

White Chameleon Poison

Nearly twenty hours passed since Ethan brought Sophia into the hospital. She was still asleep. He was beginning to worry, though the doctor assured him she would probably sleep for a while depending on how she reacted to the medicine she'd been given. Plus her body was exhausted from the violent up heaving caused by the vomiting.

Dr. Vecell gave Ethan information about the white chameleon poison and left him more confused about how she'd come in contact with it.

The plant is mostly found in the Mediterranean and could cause poisoning if eaten. Dr. Vecell told Ethan that sometimes it was mistaken for a wild artichoke, but even if that was the case, how in the world would Sophia have gotten a hold of it in Massachusetts or New York for that matter? According to the tests, Sophia's poisoning was definitely from being ingested.

Unfortunately, there was no cause to alert the police since Ethan was not aware of a motive. They would just have to wait until she woke. He refused to leave her. It was confusing enough for her to wake up at his house, but to wake up in the hospital with no one to explain why she was there, would be terrifying.

Ethan's back was stiff from sitting in the uncomfortable chair all day and night. He was glad, however, that she had a private room. Dixon offered to move her to a room that provided more comfort for visitors, but Ethan declined. He already felt as if he was in his debt for intervening on Sophia's behalf with the doctor.

Sophia, Dixon's kindness, and even being asked to stand up for Landon alongside his brother, Joshua, were distractions from a plan he'd long since put into play.

Ethan looked towards Sophia lying seemingly lifeless in the hospital bed with an IV attached to her arm, and for the millionth time, wished things were different.

He took a deep breath, leaned his head back on the chair and ran both hands down the length of his face, stopping to scratch the stubble on his chin and jaw line. It itched terribly.

"I need to shave," he said to himself.

"You look like I feel and that aint't that good at all." Her voice was raspy, but Ethan's head shot up, pleased to know she was awake.

He popped out of the chair and rushed to the bed. She frowned and looked confused as if her surroundings were slowly becoming apparent to her.

"You're in the hospital." Ethan answered her unspoken question.

Sophia looked around the bed, saw the IV and followed the tube to her arm. She looked at Ethan again.

"Every time I wake up in a strange place, I open my eyes and see you."

"So you remember waking up at my place yesterday morning?" He asked.

"Yesterday?" She lifted her head and looked around the room. She stared at the window "How long have I been here?"

"You've just been here over night."

With her head back on the pillow and her eyes closed, she asked, "What happened? Was I that drunk?" She opened her eyes and stared up at him. "Alcohol poisoning?"

Ethan wasn't sure what to tell her. He didn't want to freak her out by telling her about the poisoning, but felt that he needed to so he could get some answers.

"When you didn't respond to me after a while when I knocked on the bathroom door, I went inside and found you covered in blood."

"I remember the blood, but nothing else." She whispered.

"That's because you were unconscious when I found you. I scooped you up and brought you straight here." She waited for him to continue. "The doctor said there were traces of toxins from a plant normally found in the Mediterranean in your blood."

She frowned. "What?"

"That was my thoughts exactly."

"I…I don't understand." She seemed to be wide awake and completely confused.

Ethan told her about the plant and how a person could be poisoned from it.

"Do you have any idea how you could have ingested it?"

"No."

"Well what did you eat yesterday?"

She thought for a moment. "I don't know. I can't remember."

"What do you mean, you can't remember? Don't you know what you ate or where you ate it?" His voice rose out of frustration, but she had no way of knowing the reason. All she knew was that he sounded as if he was scolding her.

"Why are you yelling at me? I just woke up in a fuckin' hospital bed and you're interrogating me about what I had for lunch!"

Her hand slowly rubbed her throat as her chest heaved up and down. The exchange was exhausting.

"I'm sorry Sophia. I didn't mean to upset you." He wanted to reach for her hand but didn't dare. Their history was way too unstable for even simple physical contact. "Do you think you're feeling up to taking down some water?"

She'd turned away from him.

"I said, I'm sorry."

"Can you please take your sorry ass out of here and leave me the hell alone like you've done every other time we've been in the same room?"

"Sophia I—"

"Just go."

She wouldn't look at him and Ethan had no idea what to say to her. It was his fault, he knew, but not just today. She was right. He'd ignored her since the moment he found out she was Landon's best friend. In his mind, he was protecting her, but when he viewed himself from her perspective, he was a grade A ass.

Now here she was, alone, away from home, in the hospital with a man who'd upset her when she was weak and vulnerable.

"Your purse is in the drawer. I'm sorry for going through it, but I had to get information about you from your driver's license, because I know so little about you." He thought he heard her mumble, *"Who's fault is that?"* but he ignored her. It was most definitely his fault and he knew it.

"I'm leaving my card here on the side table if there is anything you need." He placed his business card next to the telephone.

She still refused to look at him.

"I'm sure you won't use it, but..." He didn't finish his statement; he simply turned and walked out of the hospital room.

This was not part of his plan. *She* was not part of his plan. He'd wondered how the whole "Sophia scene" would play out and how it would interfere with his other arrangements, however, when she dismissed him from her room she was giving him an "out" to continue as normal.

Why then, did he feel so disappointed? Sophia was a problem for him and he knew it. That truth didn't mask or take away the regret.

Unfortunately his problem began long before they flirted over a drink. Long before he knew she was Landon's best friend. Unfortunately the soft curly hair that smelled of flowers long ago had only brushed against his cheek in his dreams.

His problem had a solution but *she* was not a part of it. *She couldn't be.*

His mind told him to get the hell out of there but his feet stopped at the nurses' station. The lights in the hallway were dimmed. Even the lights over the counter only illuminated the work area of the nurses—where he found himself standing instead of walking away.

"Excuse me." Ethan addressed one of the three nurses bent over stacks of charts. She either didn't hear him or was ignoring him.

"Excuse me." He said again, louder this time.

The light from the desk seemed to shine directly into her eyes when she looked up with a frown.

"Hi." He said. "Sorry to disturb you." He figured they were used to getting their paperwork done before dawn arrived and everyone began to wake up.

When the nurse's eyes landed on Ethan, her irritated frown quickly became a solicitous toothy grin.

"Hello." She said, dragging the word out in two syllables, much too long for a professional response.

Ethan was used to women overtly flirting with him, but it still annoyed him from time to time. This was one of those times.

"Do you have any popsicles?" Ethan asked the woman. Even as he asked, he still silently berated himself for not walking out of the door and continuing his life as he'd planned. Though somehow he couldn't make himself walk away and patiently tolerated the nurse's overt perusal of him.

"Let me check. We had a kid here yesterday who got his tonsils out." She stood and straightened her clothes with exaggerated motions.

She wore purple scrubs and the top was far too tight. She pretended to cough and patted her chest lightly. "Let me just see if we have anymore." She walked out of his sight and he rolled his eyes.

From the corner of his eye he saw one of the other nurses watch her walk away and shake her head. Ethan looked at the disapproving co-worker. The woman looked at Ethan over the rim of her glasses and raised her eyebrows, as if to say, "Watch out."

The tight-topped nurse returned with an orange ice pop wrapped in a napkin.

"This is the only kind we have. Is this *all* you need?"

Ethan smiled, took the ice pop from the woman and said. "Yes, thank you so much. My *fiancé* needs something to drink but I'm not sure if she can handle water yet. This will be perfect and it's her favorite flavor."

Ethan could see the other woman put her head down and cover her mouth to conceal a giggle.

With the ice pop in hand, Ethan wondered if Sophia would even take it. He also realized he knew something about her that didn't come out of her purse. She'd mentioned something about an orange popsicle when she was dreaming the morning after her drunken night. He just hoped she didn't start throwing stuff at him when he walked back in.

Ethan eased the door open and peeked inside the room. He was shocked to find her looking at him, almost expectantly.

"I don't get you." Her voice was raspy. "You've acted like I don't exist for nearly a year and now I can't seem to get rid of you."

And as if she'd given up trying, she closed her eyes.

At least she hadn't yelled or thrown anything at him. Ethan walked in the room and stood next to the bed not responding to her statement at all. He felt it was best not to reply since he really didn't know how.

"I'm sure your mouth must feel like cotton has taken root in there." He could tell she wanted to laugh but was trying not to. "I brought this for you." She opened her eyes and he presented the ice pop. "It may be easier to get down than water right now.

She gave him a surprised reluctant smile.

She looked so tiny in the bed and the eyes that looked up at him appeared so vulnerable and frightened.

"Let me sit you up a bit." Ethan pushed the button that made the head of the bed rise. She adjusted herself and seemed to notice for the first time, the hospital gown.

"Well isn't this get-up lovely."

"It's all the rage in Paris. The runways are full of them."

Nervousness must result in corniness according to the words spilling out of his mouth.

He gave her the ice pop just to do something with his hands and hoping the distraction would keep his mouth shut. The nurse had already cut it open.

Unsure whether to sit and wait, stand or simply leave, Ethan walked over to the window. He didn't want to leave. That was apparent. The sun was rising against a clear sky. He leaned against the opening of the window with his hands in his pockets, thinking that this was the second morning he'd watched the sun rise with Sophia in the same room.

He was thinking about what would happen later in the afternoon. The doctor said they would keep her over night. Now what? Was she strong enough to travel back to New York? Where would she go? Back to the hotel or would she agree to come home with him? Did he want her to come home with him?

How had he gotten so completely involved?

Before he could contemplate the last question that clouded his mind, she called him.

"Ethan?" His name sounded so odd coming from her voice.

"Yes?" He answered as he walked to the side of the bed closest to the window.

"I can't eat any more." She handed him the uneaten portion of the pop. She'd eaten about half. He placed it in a cup next to her bed.

"How do you feel?" *Why hadn't I asked her that already? She really must think I'm an ass.*

"I feel tired and empty. Other than that, I'm ok. No pain, if that's what you're asking."

He didn't know what he was asking. He just wanted her to talk to him.

"When do I get to leave? I was only supposed to be in Boston til Sunday."

"The doctor said they were just keeping you over night as a precaution." He wanted to say more, but thought better of it. He would simply answer her questions.

"Thank you, Ethan." She placed her hands in her lap like a shy little girl.

"I'm glad I was able to help." And he really was.

She just looked at him as if deciding whether to believe him or not.

"Will you ask a nurse to come in here before you leave?"

Well, there it was. She wanted him to go.

"Sophia, I'm really not the ass you think I am. I just want to help find out how you ended up in here."

Sophia bit her bottom lip and sighed heavily. "Dear Lord, Ethan…can you just—" She started looking around the bed without finishing her statement. "Never mind, it must be here somewhere."

"What are you looking for?" Then he realized she was looking for the nurse call button. He figured she would get one of them to put him out. That's all he needed was the busty nurse to show up. "You don't have to call the nurse. I'll leave you alone."

"Damit, Ethan! It has nothing to do with you—
I need to pee!"

"Oh." His irritation eased, he found the button
and pushed it. The nurse came in right away.

Since Sophia was awake and the bag was
nearly empty anyway, they took out the IV line in her
arm and she was free to go to the bathroom without
dragging the pole with her.

The nurse didn't wait around to assist her,
either because she figured she didn't need help or
because Ethan was there with her.

Sophia's single-minded focus to get to the toilet
made her too trusting in a body that had been on its
back and devoid of sustenance, save the IV fluids, for
more than twenty-four hours. The moment her feet hit
the floor it was quite obvious what a brutal toll the
vomiting episode had put on her body. The air was
much too thin. A haze of dizziness floated around her
and pushed her from side to side, threatening to topple
her.

Ethan was immediately at her side, bracing her
with his arm tightly around her waist. Even with a head
seemingly as light as a whisper on the wind, she felt
the current of something much stronger than electricity
strangle her middle.

Seductive Pleasures

"Whoa! I wasn't expecting that!" She said not looking up at him—unsure if she meant the dizziness or the physical contact with Ethan.

She suddenly remembered the foul state of her mouth the last time she'd been conscious and wondered if it was possible for her embarrassment to be even more profound.

"Are you ok?" Her soft curly dark hair brushed against his chin and he imagined resting it on the top her head in a casual embrace. The image of them being as carefree as to stand holding each other with such ease, had his mind temporarily preoccupied.

"You, Sir, are an enigma I can't afford to contemplate right now."

Dear Lord she needed to pee.

And brush her teeth.

Ethan felt Sophia use the world-wide recognizable bounce that indicated he needed to get her to the bathroom quickly, though he was unsure of what he should do once they reached it.

She reached for the door and had to steady herself with it.

There were about six steps from the bed to the bathroom but Sophia felt like she was in one of those commercials where the person has sudden urges to urinate but none of the doors held the toilet.

This was not going to be pretty if the day had finally come when Ethan Powers recognized her as a human being and she responded by pissing all down her leg. Then she thought about the drunken night, the sunrise vomiting, the rank breath and figured peeing on herself would just be redundant.

Ethan walked into the bathroom with her, unsure if she was able to stand on her own. The bounce turned into a tight leg cross.

"Let me go, damnit!"

He let her go.

Without any outward manifestations of shame and, what seemed to happen all in one motion, she moved the gown aside, sat on the toilet and sighed in sweet relief as the dam broke free.

The quick decent on the toilet left her a bit wobbly so she consciously tried to still herself for a moment. She noticed then that Ethan had made himself scarce.

Not able to muster the strength for humiliation Sophia resigned herself to the fact that she would have to deal with Ethan Powers whether she wanted to or not.

She saw the string that would summons a nurse, but she wanted try to finish her business and exit on her own accord.

According to Ethan, the doctor was planning to release her when he came by for his morning rounds. She was tired and a little woozy, but she was sure that would pass soon. She was ready to leave the hospital.

Then what?

She hadn't let her mind think about the possibility of someone trying to harm her, but the reality of it loomed over her head like the Hindenburg dirigible.

"Do you need help getting up?"

Sophia opened the door and he stood ready to assume his post at her side. She held up a hand to still him.

"I got it Ethan." She hoped to God she did as she focused on the bed and willed her body to get there.

Anxious about making one foot go in front of the other without incident, she didn't notice her backside was on display.

However, he *did* notice.

His eyebrows lifted and his eyes danced, quite pleased with the view.

Stubborn, feisty, determined with a great ass—what a woman!

Ethan watched Sophia climb into the bed refusing his assistance.

When she was settled, she looked at him.

"I don't get it?" Before he could ask *"Get What?"* She asked another question. "How were you even able to get any medical information about me?" She shook her head trying to understand. "I mean we hardly know each other."

Ethan stuck both hands in his pocket and leaned back on the heels of his shoes, a nervous habit he thought he'd outgrown.

"I told the doctors you were my fiancé."

Her brow rose a fraction, otherwise her face showed no expression.

"You avoid me like an insurance salesman for nearly the entire year I've known you…well not known you, because I know very little about you. Which is the point I'm trying to make." He wondered if she breathed when she talked.

"Now, I'm suddenly your fiancé." She paused and held his gaze. "That isn't odd to you, Ethan?" A faint threat of hysteria was in her voice.

"I did what I needed to do. There was no one else and I was worried." It sounded simple enough to him.

She knew he was right, but she didn't know why he'd bothered to take her back to his place anyway. Well, he'd explained that, but still! Sophia wanted to be angry with Ethan but couldn't find the grounds. Truthfully, his actions were noble and could possibly have saved her life.

So she let it go.

"When are we getting married?"

Without skipping a beat he smiled, "In exactly forty-four days." Relieved she was not haranguing him about his past treatment of her.

She raised a brow.

"Counting down, are we?"

"Absolutely!"

"Just so I won't be caught off guard if someone on the hospital staff asks me about my future husband, I better gather some pertinent facts about you."

"Ok." He said while pulling the chair closer to the bed, but deciding not to sit just yet. "Fire away."

"If you were a wild animal, what would you be?"

Ethan's brows nearly pressed together in confusion and a bit of intrigue.

"Who's going to ask you that?"

"You never know. I want to be prepared for anything."

"Ok. Ok…" He tilted his head in an exaggerated thoughtful expression then looked back at her with a playful smile that was so infectious she couldn't help but smile too.

"Do I get to ask questions as well?"

She thought a moment and couldn't help the curiosity that bubbled into a giddy girly grin. "Yes. Now stop stalling. Answer the question."

"I would say…hmmm…a lion."

Sophia sucked her teeth as she rolled her eyes. "Figures…"

Ethan frowned again, feeling the playful mood evaporating.

"Figures, what?" He asked.

"Sounds just like you to want to be the *king of the jungle*."

His piercing dark eyes held hers a moment before he stated, "First of all, you just said you didn't know anything about me so your annoyance is not justified." He held her gaze until he saw the "touché" in her eyes and the terse nod of her head.

"Yes, he is the king of the jungle, but the lion is also humble enough to have a mate who is as fierce as him. Without her, he would not eat." Jauntily he cocked his curly black head to one side. "So you see, my dear fiancé, a lion has to be strong enough to support a strong woman and know that he must treat such a woman like a queen."

He bowed gallantly.

What the hell could she possible say to that?

Ethan sat in the chair and tried not to look as smug as he felt.

What he'd said was true. As far as he was concerned, a man had to be the king of the jungle to be able to handle an independent, feisty woman who could rip the teeth out of a wildebeest just for the hell of it.

He looked at Sophia lying in bed and all he could see was the strength of a lioness.

He wanted her.

The private admission slammed into him like a bolder and nearly knocked the wind out of his lungs. He'd been seduced by the prospect of deep seeded revenge for so long that he'd failed to see other prospects right in his face.

Was revenge really worth not having her?

Was he willing to find out?

He wanted her in his life, though he finally had to admit to himself that he'd been seduced by Sophia Ilarraza from the first moment he saw her crying in the cemetery.

Chapter 6

Business Ethan

Tired of being in bed, Sophia decided to wander around the house. She hadn't had a chance to look around since he practically forced her to come home with him by threatening to call Landon.

Sophia knew that was the last thing Landon needed to think about with Candice's mom being sick so close to the wedding. She'd agreed to return to his home, but adamantly refused to discuss her medical diagnosis with him.

The possibility that she may have been poisoned weighed heavily on her mind, but the entire situation was complicated enough and she didn't need Ethan's speculations or interference. The doctor assured her that death from the toxins was unlikely, but as in her case, they were capable of causing a person to become violently ill.

Sophia staunchly refused at first but then slowly became intrigued with the prospect of finding out a little more about the man who'd changed so suddenly towards her.

So she'd relented.

Exhaustion found her when she'd first arrived at Ethan's, but she was beginning to feel like herself again. She no longer felt weak, nauseous or lightheaded, which meant she could make her return flight to New York on Sunday.

Sunday.

Two whole days away. Could she stay with Ethan for two days?

It was barely two in the afternoon and already she'd gone to the hotel so they could retrieve her things, forced down chicken broth from a deli near the hospital and taken a nap.

The hospital released her in record time. In all of her thirty-six years, she'd never known anyone who didn't have to wait until congress convened to get checked out of the hospital.

However, when Dr. Vecell arrived at promptly eight o'clock, a nurse accompanied him. He pushed her belly, checked her eyes and pulse then was on his way after he addressed with Ethan strict orders to call him if the vomiting returned or if she was still lethargic by Sunday. She looked at Ethan with a cocked eyebrow. Ethan assured the doctor that he would and shook his hand, coolly ignoring the cocked pistol aimed at his head.

The doctor tucked his pen light in his coat pocket and walked out of the room. The nurse had her sign the release documents, said she would return in a moment with the wheel chair and within a few moments she was there locking the wheels so Sophia could climb into her exit chariot.

There was nothing to gather. She'd arrived at the hospital in a pair of leggings and a blood-soiled camisole. And she probably would have been discharged in the leggings and the fancy backless gown if not for Ethan. After he'd helped her to the restroom he said he would be right back—there was something he had to do. He returned with three Wal-Mart shopping bags. Even if she hadn't thought about her exit gear, he had. Sophia was extremely touched by his thoughtfulness.

Inside one of the bags were a set of pink cotton sweats, a pair of ankle-high white socks, a pair of blue cotton panties and pink slippers. Her brows gathered when she looked up at him.

"I didn't think to grab your shoes."

"Oh." Her voice was soft as she thought about the scene he must have walked in on and the panic he experienced of having a woman covered in blood unconscious at the base of his toilet.

Seductive Pleasures

The other bags contained toiletry items she desperately needed. She didn't dare think what mess lay atop her head and well, the breath situation, that was a different story altogether.

She was grateful and she told him so.

"Thank you Ethan." She said looking into the bags. Sophia slowly raised her eyes to him. "For everything."

By 8:15 am, she, her purse, a bag of toiletries and her new pink outfit and slippers were all seated in Ethan's car. That had to be a miracle she thought, to be checked out so quickly, and on the drive mentioned it to Ethan. He informed her that Dr. Vecell was a friend of Dixon's which probably helped her quick departure. She'd been confused so he had to relay the entire story with Dr. Patel and his poor attitude.

"So it wasn't a miracle; it was a Phoenix...Sounds about right."

She noticed the tight set of his jaw before she turned to view the buildings stretching to the sunshine against the blue sky.

"Did you change the numbers like I asked?...Good...Fax the new documents to Franklin's lawyer... Right...Call a meeting for 10am Monday

…That's all the time he's getting! Trust me, he'll take it. He doesn't have a choice."

Ethan walked to the door of his office and looked down the hallway then walked back into the room.

Sophia had taken about five steps away from the guestroom when she heard his voice shatter the silence of his spacious home. It rang with the confidence of a man who was used to taking charge, not because of his authority, but because he knew exactly what he was doing and how to do it.

On the dance floor there was nothing sexier than a man who knew how to take the lead and still let the woman move freely and seductively around him. No matter how feisty or independent Sophia portrayed herself to be, she loved a man who knew how to adeptly handle the reins. But she also knew there was a fine line between taking charge when needed and being controlling.

She wished she could distract herself from listening to him by looking at pictures on the hallway walls, but there were none. Just empty space
… and his voice.

Sophia cursed the arousal snaking its way through parts of her that had been dormant for far too long.

Seductive Pleasures

Traitorous…traitorous body!

Her eyes narrowed and focused on the part of the house where his voice lured her like a cat to curiosity. And everyone knows what happened to the cat.

He was clearly busy but her feet kept moving forward. She wanted to see him. Wanted to observe the lines of his face and the set of his jaws when he delegated, directed or dictated, she didn't care which.

Her chest rose and fell, pushing out short audible breaths.

What the hell was wrong with her?

It had to be residual effects of the poisoning.

Normally a man needed to physically touch her to bring her into arousal. So the mere fact that Ethan's voice could inflame her was…well…startling and frankly…dangerous.

Sophia wanted to be his lioness—to sharpen her claws in a heated dispute, drag them along his back until he cried out in pleasure and their limbs became as tangled as a climbing vine on a tree.

She'd never heard him in action.

Not like this.

To her, he'd only showed indifference. To others in her circle, he was easy going and funny. This Ethan that she heard on the phone—this *business*

Ethan was unfamiliar and she could hardly contain her lioness growl that rumbled just below the surface. Her reaction shocked and exhilarated her.

What would it be like to dance with him in bed? What would it be like to seduce or be seduced by Ethan Powers? To have his hands splayed across her backside? To have him so near her that his heat seared the nipples of her breasts. What would it be like to dig her fingers in the unruly curls of his ebony hair while getting lost in the dizziness of his kisses?

She'd heard the rumors. He'd been in Boston only a short time but it didn't take long for women to talk. Her new friend, Alex was privy to lots of town gossip when she sometimes worked at Cliques. And the town gossip was that Ethan Powers was known for two things—his brilliant business mind and his perfect penis. Though, the latter had come from a hussy who tried to trap him into getting her pregnant, it didn't matter, the intrigue still prevailed.

"Let me worry about that. Phoenix doesn't have a leg to stand on... Yes... I said let me worry about that...I'm handling the deal...Phoenix won't know the difference...It's going to ruin him!"

Ethan disconnected the call without another word. Her feet halted and head swirled with questions.

*What did he mean, "It's going to ruin him!"
Ruin who?*

She heard Ethan shuffling papers in what she figured was his office.

First, arousal, now this. What was this?

She was even more confused. Which Phoenix was he talking about? Landon?

Before, Sophia's uncertainty about Ethan stemmed from his frosty attitude towards her. She'd never questioned anything else about him, because everyone else seemed to be crazy about him.

For goodness sakes, Landon asked Ethan to be in his wedding.

Who was Ethan Powers and was he friend or foe?

Here she was sauntering through a man's house, wearing a pink outfit she'd never even considered buying, sleeping in his guestroom, and she had no idea who he was.

She realized that she didn't really know him at all. They'd talked briefly that one night, but what can you truly find out about a person through a series of shameless flirting? She did, however, remember that he said he could sing and play the piano. Could he really or was that sexy bar banter? Either way it didn't contribute to a person's character, not in the long run.

Sophia didn't know if she should leave or try to find out more about him.

Frustration and the realization that she didn't have her rental car, moved her feet faster towards the office. How did her life become so complicated in just two days?

He knew she was there before he turned. Her scent had been imbedded into his brain for two years and now it filled every space of his home. He didn't mind. It was time he gave up fighting.

Yes, he wanted her.

He wanted to argue with her until she ignited into a ball of passion and exploded all over him.

He wanted to let go of the anger he held and the revenge he sought against a family who'd taken him in and treated him like…well, like…family.

What would they say if they knew who he truly was?

Ethan didn't get a chance to let the question develop and play out in his mind before she spoke.

"I heard you on the phone." Sophia stated plainly.

Ethan turned to face her.

"My apologies for disturbing you, I was going to check on you in a moment."

"You didn't disturb me." His eyes held her gaze so intently and his words were as soft and soothing, that her haughtiness lost a bit of its edge. "I wasn't asleep."

"Oh?"

Swallowed in the pink sweats made her feel small and as soft as a spool of cotton candy. His eyes were melting the frozen waters of her delta just as easily as a tongue melts the sweet strands of finely spun sugar. The new panties were definitely in danger of impending moisture. What the hell was wrong with her?

"Are you ok?"

"What?" She blinked and refocused on him as if seeing him for the first time.

"Here. Sit down, Sophia. You're supposed to be resting. Are you feeling dizzy."

God help her. She *was* dizzy, but it had nothing to do with recovering from being in the hospital. It had everything to do with Ethan Powers standing a foot and a half away from her, etched in confidence and exuding the epitome of his last name. She took a deep breath, looked down and tried to gain some confidence of her own.

Not only was it none of her business, who or what he was talking about, but she was constantly

93

afraid that he would return to the Ethan who ignored her.

"I'm fine, Ethan." And she really was. Compared to how she'd felt the morning of the hangover.

Sophia looked directly at him. "I heard you on the phone and it sounded like you were scheming behind Landon's back." There was no need in skirting around the subject.

Standing taller, she added, "Who the hell are you, Ethan and what are you up to?"

"I'm Joshua and Landon's older brother."

Stunned, all she could do was stare at him.

Was he kidding? No. Why would he make up something like that? Still unable to speak, she dragged her eyes from his feet to his head and just as if she'd put on glasses, she saw him clearly. He bore the light coloring of Landon's skin tone, Joshua's curly black hair, the height and nose of both the other brothers.

Brothers?

She could tell he was searching her face trying to read her thoughts. For a reason she couldn't fathom, he gave her an apologetic smile. There it was. The smile was an exact replica of Josh and Landon's.

But how? Did they know?

"Say something?" He uttered in a harsh whisper.

There were so many things she wanted to say but the only words that traveled from her brain and made their way to her mouth were, "What was that phone call about?" She had to know.

He leaned casually against the front of his desk with his hands loosely holding the edge. She hated that he was so sexy even in just a simple light blue t-shirt and jeans and his relaxed look made him appear even more confidant.

"Business."

The word was naked of any emotion—as frigid and unexpected as a skater disappearing through the ice on a pond.

The atmosphere in the room was instantaneously chilly.

There he was. The Ethan she knew—the one who raised her ire. The one she'd hoped not to see a gain.

Heat suddenly shot up her neck singeing her face. Her eyes blazed. She wanted to slap him for making her believe she was wrong about him—for making her think he may have cared a little about her and for all the things she didn't know about him.

Sophia wanted to slap him for making her feel giddy when she put on the pink warm ups, knowing he'd picked them out for her. She wanted to slap the hell out of him because she didn't know why his attitude pissed her off. She especially wanted to slap him because of the heat pooling at the meeting of her thighs.

So she did.

The tiny sound of her hand smacking his face only echoed her frustrations, but the moment her palm connected with his flesh, currents ricocheted through her and every nerve in her body sung with anticipation, need and longing.

Ethan stood unmoving. His eyes held her.

The darkening of his eyes was not supposed to harden her nipples and tug the nerves in the apex of her thighs—that too pissed her off.

She slapped him again and spat out,

"How dare you!"

He said nothing, just held her with those eyes of his that beckoned a side of her that few men could handle. He stepped towards her.

She tried not to let his nearness affect her.

"How dare you slip back behind that ice mask of yours!" She took a tentative step back at first, and then stood straighter. Confidently, she took a step towards him as if she matched him in size, instead of standing a foot shorter and several pounds lighter.

Ethan blinked, suddenly stepped to the side and with a determined, stride made for the door.

That confused her, but she reacted quickly.

"Oh no you don't." She said as she scrambled to the door and shut it before he reached it.

With her back resting against his exit and her breast rising and falling in earnest, she faced him again.

"What are you about, Ethan? Are you trying to sabotage Landon?"

Those eyes again. Deep, dark and dangerous. His head tilted to one side as he whispered the single word in defeat, "No."

Betrayed by the breath that hesitated her voice, she faltered. Sophia didn't have time to defend herself from what she knew was coming and what she knew she would not be able to resist. Anger exploded inside of her and because of it, the fire ignited a flame of desire so blistering she couldn't control it if she tried.

So she didn't.

She was immediately engulfed.

Chapter 7

Losing Control

Desire ripped a jagged hole in his control. His need was maddening, carnal, raw and absolutely necessary for his survival. He'd tried to escape it and her. She placed herself in front of him. The grip on the rope he'd held to keep his control in place burned his hands as it sped ferociously from its grasp. Sophia was the balm he needed to soothe them. He literally ached to touch her.

With her back pressed against the wall, his hands sought her waist and lifted her. His mouth immediately found hers. A low growl escaped her partially opened lips and then she bit him—not in protest but with a need just as great as his. He'd known she would be ferocious.

The light metallic taste of the blood from his lip quickly faded as he drove greedily into her mouth and kissed her fervently trying to embed the taste of her into his tongue.

He noticed with Sophia that desire was not sweet and romantic; it was fierce, dangerous and uncontrollable. It was hot.

Ethan tried to burn a trail of desire wherever his tongue touched. Her lips, her neck, her ears, the base of her jaw. Sophia's legs had long since wrapped around his waist. He slid her along the hardness of his erection and she moaned with what sounded like anticipation to him.

His voice thick and unsteady, he revealed his need, unable to stop tasting her. "I've got to have you." His voice simmered with unchecked passion. "This moment."

She replied by dragging her teeth along the flesh of his neck and pressing into his erection. That was all the affirmation he needed.

He held her with one hand and freed himself from his jeans with the other. Placing both hands under her round bottom and sandwiching her between him and the door, he steadied her and himself as he freed his feet from the jeans.

Ethan let her slide along the door until his hardness rested on the soft cotton covering the apex of her thighs.

"Please Ethan." Was the strangled plea.

That was his undoing. She was pleading for him. She wanted him as much as he wanted her. With a motion that should have been caught on camera for proof it was not magic, he released her, quickly pulled her free from the pink sweats and panties and lifted her again.

His tongue was not yet done branding her. With ease, he lifted her until her legs rested on his shoulders. He felt her brace herself by locking her hands around his head, knowing what was coming. His eyes met the main course and he did not delay in his feasting.

She was completely waxed.

Mercy.

The moment his tongue penetrated her folds he knew he would never tire of the taste of her. With his eyes closed, he let his tongue travel the length of her opening—dipping, licking, tasting and discovering every delectable part of her womanly core. Never had a woman drove him to such frenzy. Never had he gotten such pleasure by giving pleasure. And by the moans and low growls coming from Sophia, he knew she was enjoying it as much as he. Every erotic sound that purred or roared from her only intensified his need. His entire body was rigid with it. Every maddening lick pushed him higher and faster to an edge of a magnificent cliff.

Her increasing wetness, tensing of her thigh muscles and the powerful grip she had on his head and hair let him know her climax was on the horizon.

Seductive Pleasures

Ethan squeezed Sophia's hips as he prepared
for her undoing. The tip of his tongue sought her
harden nodule and he sucked and plied her place of
pleasure until she filled his office with some Spanish
words he didn't know and the sound of his name
vibrating against the walls, followed by an intense
shudder from her thighs.

Again, with the stealth of a magician, Ethan
captured the last of her verbal pleasures with his mouth
as the orgasm rocketed through her and at the same
moment he impaled the tightness of her core; he knew
his own undoing would not take long.

Glory be to the gods, she was exquisite.

She held on to him as if she wanted to press
their souls together. To Ethan, that's exactly what their
joining felt like—the mingling of two souls in
desperate need of each other. Their coming together
was spontaneous, explosive, and wild—and seemed
completely right.

Against the door of his office, he mated with a
woman with an intensity that frightened the hell out of
him, but he needed it like he needed air.

"No te detengas!" Sophia yelled, gripped his
back and met him thrust for glorious thrust. He had no
idea what she said but, whatever it was after a few
more thrusts, she screamed his name so loudly, he was

sure it could be heard in Concord. He could feel her core throbbing around the length of him and it triggered his own orgasm. He had to grit his teeth to try and stifle the exquisite cry that threatened to escape him. It did not help. He voiced a blend of her name and a growl as the intensity of his release rammed through him with such force it nearly buckled his knees.

As the insane moment came to a sated end, he realized he'd just released inside of her.

Never had he been so blinded by wanting a woman that he'd forgotten to protect them with a condom. It was too late now. The deed was done.

Within a small window of time, he'd revealed who he was and gotten totally addicted to a woman whom he'd told himself over and over was a bad idea.

He waited for sanity to settle back into place, but it didn't and he wondered if it ever would.

Both naked from the waist down and still inside of her, he walked to his small sofa and sat with her straddling him. He was afraid to look into her eyes. Afraid to see regret resting there. He looked anyway.

What he saw surprised and aroused him. He could feel himself coming alive inside of her again. How was that possible? He'd just had an orgasm that matched none other and he could feel himself thickening inside of her.

This was pure madness.

Sophia's body surged and gloried in the aftermath of their sex. She'd heard about the effects of crack on first time users. It was said that the high was so good and powerful, that they spent the rest of their addiction in pursuit of that first high.

After one hit, she was addicted and just had to know if it was a fluke and if she could get that same high again. Fear coiled its way up her spine because Ethan Powers unleashed a hunger within her and she wasn't sure how to rein it in. Hell, she didn't want it reined in, but she also knew that she didn't want him to have any sort of hold on her. She was strong but she wasn't sure if she could fight against the urges to be completely immersed by him.

But for now, she didn't want to fight it. She wanted that high again.

The moment he looked at her, Sophia wanted more. A feline smile spread across her face and she breathed, "Dame más." As she gently rocked her hips and flexed her feminine walls.

Again, Ethan had no idea what she said, but didn't give a damn. He watched her face darken with desire and he pulled off her sweat shirt. He wanted to see her breasts rise and fall as she breathed deeply. He wanted to feel her breasts in his hands and discover how her nipples would react to his tongue.

He was giving her what she wanted whether he knew the words or not. She'd loved being taken against the door. Never in her life had a man made love to her standing. It exhilarated her. It was wild— free. She felt liberated.

When he removed her top she couldn't wait to feel his hands on her skin. They scorched a path of carnal lust as they traveled along her torso and the moment he pinched a nipple her body splintered.

Not letting her recover, Ethan held her hips and guided her into a riding motion. It didn't take long before she'd taken over and was riding him like she was trying to break a wild stud. She grabbed his shoulders and slid her nails along his arms.

What kind of power does this man possess to elicit such wonton behavior from me?

Ethan couldn't stop touching her. He didn't caress her skin; he grabbed and stroked her with such force he worried if he would leave bruises. She didn't seem to mind, in fact she appeared even more aroused.

She rode him hard. He felt as if he couldn't get close enough to her and he was no small man. Not many women could take the entire length of him so he was elated when she seemed to relish taking him in to the hilt. Still he felt as if he wanted her closer. He wanted them to melt together and mingle in a way he'd never done with another woman. He didn't understand it, but would have to think about it later. Right now, he wanted ever molecule to concentrate on the woman astride him.

"Sophia. Sophia. Sophia." He moaned her name over and over and the sound of it drove her to ride harder.

Ethan couldn't get enough of her sweet dark nipples and areolas which contrasted sharply against her light skin tone that blended with his own. He licked, teased and nibbled and knew he would never get his fill. Her breasts were full with a heaviness that made them extremely sexy without being overtly obvious in her clothes. The scent of her was so surreal because for the longest time it was only a memory. Now here he was, nestled between her breasts inhaling it from a very tangible woman.

Sophia shifted a bit and began bouncing quickly then slowing with a control he thanked the heavens for, she guided herself along the entire length of him from the base to the head and back. She rode him so painstakingly slow that he was sure the delectable torture would kill him. Bolts of electricity surged from the bottom of his feet to his earlobes.

105

They too, tingled and burned in anticipation of his undoing.

"You're killing me, Baby." He managed through gritted teeth.

Sophia smiled and raised her brows as she toyed with the head of his erection with her moist opening. Unable to take it any longer, Ethan grabbed her hips and quickly impaled her to the hilt.

Sophia raised a finger and waged it from side to side. Her features darkened and arousal choked him with anticipation.

Punishing him for terminating her sweet torture, she quickly put her feet on the sofa for leverage and began plunging him in and out of her with a tempo that would shatter them both quickly. His hands on her hips were hot and sure as he helped guide his missile for a perfect explosive impact. She abandoned herself to the whirl of sensation and was completely seduced by the current that seemed to arc between them. Her body vibrated from liquid fire and she erupted as she rode the waves of an orgasm that rivaled the first they'd shared. Her bones melted as she collapse against his chest. Their heartbeats and breathing filled the space.

As Sophia tried to return back to earth she suddenly felt empathetic towards crack-heads.

Ethan couldn't control the strangled outcry of ecstasy as his own release followed Sophia's. Breathing heavily, still locked together, he knew his world would never be the same. Twice he'd been so caught up in their fiery passion that he'd released inside of her. That was not like him. He was not himself when she was around.

They had a lot to talk about—the poisoning, his true identity, the fact that he'd released his seed inside of her and what they would do now.

Chapter 8

Addicted

"Did I do that?" She asked pointing to his lip.

Ethan dragged his tongue across his slightly swollen bottom lip.

"It's nothing."

Sophia ran a gentle finger across it and he felt a twinge in his groin.

"Sorry."

"No need to apologize. I loved every second." And he had.

Still astride him, though no longer engaged, she sat up.

"So did I." Whereas before she was bold and brazen, now she felt shy and quiet.

"Did I do *that*?" He asked with alarm as he ran his hands along her side and hips.

The vixen in her stirred as she watched his hands caress the red marks that showed the aggressiveness of their love making.

"It's nothing." She echoed.

Ethan looked up into the beautiful face with big brown eyes that haunted him in his sleep. He twirled a finger through one of her short ebony locks.

"We need to talk."

"I know."

His palm rested on her cheek and he held her gaze.

"About *everything*."

"I know." Sophia knew the *everything* included the questions about the poisoning. She also had questions of her own, but would rather talk when she was dressed.

"Can I shower and get dressed first or do you prefer me like this."

Ethan smiled that sly Phoenix smile she'd seen on Landon so many times. Why hadn't she ever noticed it before? Did everyone know but her?

"I prefer you like this, but I'll let you get dressed first. I have a feeling that if we don't we will never finish our discussion."

Sophia waved mockingly, "Talking is so overrated."

Ethan was tempted to call her bluff, but knew they needed to talk.

"You'd rather bite me instead?"

A seductive veil covered her eyes and he could feel his manhood stir to life again. "Go on woman before you kill me with your beguiling ways."

She smiled, raised an eyebrow, but slowly peeled herself off of him to stand. She felt a little weak from all the activity but knew it had been worth it. She gathered her clothes from the floor and sauntered out of the room epitomizing the movements and grace of an accomplished dancer...and lioness

Ethan dragged his hands down his face when she disappeared from view. Sophia Ilarraza was some kind of woman.

What the hell had happened? She'd gone in his office to demand answers and give him a piece of her mind and instead had ended up giving him a piece of her ass. How in the hell did that happen? But just as the question floated from one side of her mind to the other, she knew the answer.

From the first moment she saw him at Clique's, she'd wanted him. His playful smile and sensual eyes made him friendly enough to want to find out more. His confident stride and manner along with his quick mind and scandalous conversation made her want to take him to bed. Her hopes of making him part of her frequent visits to Boston were dissolved once Ethan found out she was Landon's friend. She released a long sigh.

Seductive Pleasures

In the guest bathroom, Sophia looked around
and found it appeared to be a normal bathroom that
housed all the basic white fixtures. The shower curtain
and rugs were black and there were fluffy white towels
on a shelf near the pedestal sink. She'd looked in the
medicine cabinet behind the only mirror in the space to
find it too, held the basics—cotton swabs, a couple
toothbrushes in the packages, dental floss and
toothpaste.

She reached behind the shower curtain to start
the shower and as the steam fogged the mirror she tried
to make herself see Ethan with a bit more clarity. Yes,
they needed to talk. Even if it meant she had to tell him
about the man stalking her.

Could he really have poisoned her? Until now,
she'd thought he was simply a client who'd taken his
crush on her to another level. The letter she'd received
before she left Manhattan was distressing, but again,
she tossed it from her mind thinking about spending
time with Alexandra and Candice. Now she wasn't so
sure if the man was harmless.

Sophia stepped into the shower and let the hot
stream of water wash away all the questions and
worries. Instead, she focused on Ethan, the man. The
man who'd awakened her suppressed sexual desire. It
had been a very long time since she'd found a man

who'd sparked her interest not to mention inflame her enough to want to bed. It was one of the reasons why she'd shunned monogamy; the thought of being exclusive with only one man seemed as boring as a convent with a vow of silence. Avoiding any type of long term relationship and not finding a man who'd made her warm, let alone hot, had led her to an unintentional state of celibacy.

Ethan had taken her against the door. It wasn't a dream. It wasn't one of her fantasies she'd played out in her head. It was real.

Ethan Powers had taken her against the door. The thought kept replaying in her head. It took everything she could muster not to come apart the moment he'd let her feel his hardness through her sweats. It was like something out of the movies…and it had happened to *her*…with *him*.

Mentally checking it off of her fantasy to-do list, she marveled at how even the memory made her nipples harden with wanting.

Maybe the hot water was not a good idea after all. She was getting turned on all over again. She thought of the crack-head once more and pictured herself in some sort of group discussion introducing herself and admitting her addiction.

"I'm Sophia Ilarraza and I'm addicted to Ethan Powers."

Heaven help her; she needed divine intervention.

With the dampness of the fresh shower clinging to her hair and the lingering effects of the explosive sex-apade, Sophia padded in bare feet into Ethan's living room. It was the first real opportunity she had to look around since he brought her to his home.

The first thing she noticed was the beautiful shiny black piano. She loved the curves of it. It held court in the corner of the spacious room. Somehow it fit, she didn't mean in the space, but it seemed to fit Ethan. She didn't find it odd at all to find a baby grand in his living room. Of course she just had to touch it.

Tink...tink...tink...

The chirp of the key was light and happy. She lifted her head. What was that sound? There was a warm crackled hum filling the air that was surprisingly familiar. Stepping away from the piano, her eyes brushed over the modest leather furniture and imagined herself sinking into the large overstuffed brown sofa at the end of a long day.

Sophia tried to picture Ethan lounging on the sofa with his feet up watching TV, but the image would not take root in her mind. Ethan's sometimes arctic demeanor just would not allow her to envision him as a regular guy. Although, that thought led her to remembering how powerful he'd sounded on the phone earlier.

Thinking of the conversation she'd overheard brought back her confrontation with him—though the confrontation was more of a consummation. He'd totally consumed her.

Aggressive, controlling, confident and so totally thorough.

She'd dreamt about getting taken against a door since she was old enough to have such fantasies.

Pausing for a moment in her search of the noise that hovered over the room, she remembered the day she and her friend Selena found a video tape left in the VCR—"Handsome and Gretchen." She and Selena turned and looked at each other in confusion, totally naïve to the play on words.

They were seventeen.

They'd put the tape back in the VCR and quickly surmised the tape most likely belonged to Selena's older brother, Jorge. Selena hastily moved to take it out after seeing the character deemed as "Handsome" stand behind bars and have the "witch" stroke his privates to check for the proper firmness.

Seductive Pleasures

Sophia stopped her friend and stared mesmerized as Handsome was released. The witch commanded sex and he proceeded to take her against a gingerbread wall.

The set was crappy and the gingerbread walls were clearly wallpapered to look like gingerbread. The acting was robotic at best, but it was the most erotic thing Sophia had ever seen. Her body had hummed and ignited with a need foreign to her.

Her boyfriend, Hector had never elicited such a feeling. At seventeen she was no longer a virgin, but she had no idea sex was so wild and carnal or that just watching it could make her feel so alive. All she'd known was the unrefined groping from Hector. She'd never even had the urge to touch "it."

She was seventeen, a senior in high school, and most of her friends were having sex. Many of the girls were already planning their weddings. It was their culture. Girls grew up to marry. Hector's family were good friends with hers and she knew that eventually she would marry as well.

After seeing the video she was captivated by the idea of the type of sex that made a woman moan and cry out in pleasure. She wondered if her own brother had a stash of porn and searched for it the next chance she got—he did and she watched them whenever she got the chance.

Was it so weird that the videos fascinated her? To her, they were simply learning tools. Her mom sure as hell hadn't told her anything about sex and her friends knew no more than she.

Hector no longer excited her. She wanted someone who made her writhe with pleasure like the women in the videos, though she found that none of her friends had sex lives different from hers. She began to wonder if the movies were just made up fantasies.

Until she met Manuel and found out they were. Real passion was so much better. It wasn't forced or crass—it was mind-numbing and special. With Manuel, she found out sex connected two people in a way that made them vulnerable and safe at the same time.

Sophia shook her head to release the memory of Manuel. There was too much pain hiding there.

What was that sound?

The soft scratch...scratch... still puzzled her. Her eyes traveled the room again. Nestled between two shelves filled with albums, she spotted the console. She'd heard her aunt talk about something like it, but she'd never seen one herself.

Seductive Pleasures

Sophia walked over to the consol and lifted the lid. An album was spinning but had come to an end. She picked up the needle and placed it gently at the edge of the album. Etta James "All I Could Do Is Cry" began to play and her body instinctively began to sway along with the powerful voice that filled the room.

She closed the lid and ran her fingers along the shiny dark wood that was polished to perfection. She lifted the lid again and studied the knobs. The speakers were so crisp and clear she wondered if they'd been replaced by more modern versions.

She bent down and rubbed her hand along the intricate cut of the wood camouflaging the speaker front and felt the heartbeat of the music. The subtle boom-ba-boom nearly held her in a trance.

Sophia wondered where Ethan had gotten it.

"It was my mother's. She loved music and had a closet full of vinyl albums."

Without turning, she stood and smiled. How could the man always read her mind?

"It's beautiful." She replied, still admiring the player. She noticed the almost reverent tone he used when talking about his mother. She was positive that she'd passed away and he still carried the pain of losing her—a burden she knew all too well.

117

Ethan had never let anyone touch his mother's stereo console. It was strictly off limits to the few women who'd stayed over. Though, here he was, standing by while watching Sophia explore every inch of it. For some reason he felt his mother would have liked this spirited woman.

Sophia thought the stereo was beautiful. He wanted to say, "So are you," but didn't know how to pull it off without coming off cheesy. So he simply stood and watched as she admired his mom's prized possession.

She no longer wore the pink warm up he'd so unceremoniously taken off of her. She had on a pair of jeans and a plain white t-shirt, from what he could tell from the back. Her feet were bare which pleased him to know she felt at ease enough to walk barefooted. She fit in his living room. Hell, for that matter she'd fit in his office—she fit everywhere.

Sophia had yet to face him or respond to his comment.

Was she upset with him?

He'd known she'd just been released from the hospital, but it was as if he'd been completely possessed by a greedy need to have her that moment—It was maddening, dizzying.

It was air.

Long deep inhaling of oxygen. He'd needed her like he needed to breathe. Ethan had needed to taste her, feel her, hear his name being stolen from her lips. He'd needed to see pleasure mask her face. The need to inhale her scent drove him insane. He wanted to drown himself in her essence—feed his body and maybe even his soul with all that is Sophia.

He felt his need strain against the zipper of his jeans begging to be buried within Sophia, but he knew they needed to talk.

"I guess you're ready to talk, now." Sophia turned towards Ethan and was surprised by the desire etched in his face. She also saw the outline in his jeans.

White-hot passion erupted like lava shooting from her core. It was urgent, senseless and undeniable. She couldn't contain it even if she tried. She really didn't want to try.

The heat from his reaction to her pushed her back towards the player and she used her butt to steady herself.

"You must have an even lower opinion of me than you had before." He stated.

"I've never had a low opinion of you. I just couldn't understand why you were such an asshole." She replied.

119

Were they really having this conversation *right* now? She could barely remember her name and he was involved in a discussion they could and would have later.

"Being an asshole is not having a low opinion of me?"

Dear Lord if this man didn't shut the hell up, she would kill him.

"No," is all she could manage.

He grinned, and then gently asked, "How are you feeling?"

"Other than wanting to have you take me against the door again, I feel fine."

Ethan's manhood surged to full life and his hands ached to lift her by her firm round ass and take her on his mother's beloved stereo console.

"But I feel you have a need that we should talk."

Ethan's mouth released his tongue and he somehow gathered his senses enough to remember how to use it.

"Yes."

She raised a brow. "Yes?"

Sophia watched him shift from one foot to the other. His jeans rested below his belly button and she wondered if he had a line of curly black hair that led to the goodness between his thighs. She had to admit she had not taken any time to notice before. The v-neck gray shirt currently hid that part of his body from view.

"Ethan?" She breathed, trying to capture his attention. This man was too sexy to be real, she thought. She sensed he was trying to decide between talking now or talking later. She could make it easier on him by just sitting on the sofa and insisting they get the conversation over. But why should she? He'd never made anything easy for her.

Sophia eased away from the console and dragged her eyes from Ethan's black converse up his thighs and rested briefly at the bulge in his pants. She felt her own center become moist at the sight. Walking slowly with hips swaying, she stalked towards him.

Her feet burned holes in the wood floors, fueling an intense desire that she didn't seem to have any control of. Passion hung like thick smoke choking them both, with relief coming only in the joining of their mouths. Sophia felt that if she could only kiss him, she would be able to breathe again.

She didn't want to talk about him being Landon and Joshua's brother. Hell, he could be the brother of Satan and she still wouldn't be able to defend herself from the seductive drive that was feeding her.

She wanted Ethan Powers—it was that simple. She wanted him to want her with the same intensity she'd yearned for him since they met.

Like a rabbit in a den of lions, he was defenseless. Ethan watched the way she began each step on the ball of her foot, elongating each shapely leg that the jeans hugged with perfection. She raised her chin in confident determination.

The short dark curls of her hair were sassy, cute and sexy. He noticed then that she was not wearing a bra and the tips of her nipples strained to be free from the shirt. He remembered how perfectly her breast fit in his hands and mouth. The shirt didn't reach the waist of her jeans and he saw the golden flesh of her flat belly as she strode towards him.

"Do you really want to talk?" Her words floated up and disappeared like smoke being lost in the air.

Her tongue peeked out a little as she grabbed her bottom lip with her teeth. She stood in front of him with her thumb hooked through a belt loop.

Talk? He couldn't utter a sound if he tried. He couldn't even remember the process. His mind was saturated with the taste of Sophia as her thighs rested atop his shoulders.

"Ethan?" She questioned, lifting a brow.

Seductive Pleasures

Ethan had no idea how this woman had completely taken over his good sense, but it was a question he would ponder later. He didn't remember removing her shirt, though it was gone and the air crackled against his ears as he placed one dark bud in his mouth and then the other.

If he could just get another taste of her, his mind would be free to function normally again—he was almost positive.

Her dark nipples bloomed giving evidence of how much she was enjoying his erotic ministrations.

Ethan was lost in the dizzying effects of her pleasure. She moaned his name repeatedly as if worshipping the hands that plied her pleasurably and made her pool shamelessly at the center of her womanhood.

They were still standing in the middle of his living room.

He lifted her, brought her to the sofa and sat her atop him. Ethan slowly began to open the button of the jeans and prepared to show her what he could not voice in words, only moments before.

Chapter 9

No More Small Talk

Sophia wondered if God had a color wheel and tested out how certain hues looked cast against the sky. The mixture of greens, purple and orange was unlike anything she'd ever seen made by man.

Sunrise and sunset were perfect times to try out something new. The sunrise gave hope to new possibilities and the sunset gave pause and time for reflection on opportunities gained or lost at the end of a day.

Sophia sat in the window seat off of Ethan's kitchen and reflected on the past few days while watching colors streak the horizon then fade into a rich blue then black.

She would be leaving in the morning. Pulling her legs into her chest, she hugged them. Just the thought of leaving Ethan was filling her with emptiness. They had yet to have the talk. Ethan was out picking up food. Her appetite had come back full-throttle after two days of marathon love making.

Two whole days and they were together nearly every moment of it. Early Saturday morning Ethan left for a brief meeting, but had returned with an insatiable appetite for her.

It was crazy. It only took a look, a touch, a word, or just being next to each other. The latter was proven by the closet episode.

She'd needed help getting a blanket from the closet's top shelf. As he reached to get it for her, her eyes fixated on the muscle play in his arms. Those same arms had held her up when he'd feasted at her center and made her body splinter into pieces she never got back.

When Ethan grabbed the blanket and handed it to her, desire pushed through her pores and glowed like a neon light in the dim of the closet. He must have seen it, because he dropped the blanket and took her right there against the wall of the closet, surrounded by winter outerwear and the blanket at their feet.

Heat filled her face and her breast ached with the memory. She wondered if she would ever stop craving him.

"It's that look that you have right there, that has us famished."

Ethan placed the bags he was carrying on the counter though the contents no longer interested him. The temperature seemed to rise along with other parts of him.

Seductive Pleasures

She smiled and wondered if they would ever get to eat. Getting back to New York was a necessity if only to just eat and sleep. Then it occurred to her that she still didn't know any more about Ethan than she had when he'd taken her home drunk from the sports bar.

Well...that wasn't exactly true.

She knew where he was ticklish, that he was very strong, and that he could have sex any place.

Any place.

Sophia looked at all the bags. Sadness threatened to choke her, knowing he'd bought so much just because she was there. He'd mentioned before that though he could cook, he ate out most days, because it was more convenient. Hence the reason there had been no food in his small pantry when she'd looked about an hour ago.

She cursed the tears stinging her eyes and swallowed them back, but her tight throat fought the reflex. She figured she may as well rip the bandage off in one pull.

"How about I help you whip something up before I tell you that I'm being stalked, which could possibly have something to do with the poisoning; you tell me what your deal with the Phoenix's is; and even though we've used condoms after the first few times,

126

you don't have to worry about you have gotten me pregnant."

She place her feet on the floor to stand and tried to ignore the shocked look on his face. She needed to escape the effect he had on her. Around him she was in constant danger. His mere presence dissolved her ability to use her brain. She knew she'd been functioning on pure feelings and her feelings were raw attraction—unchecked and uncensored.

It was time she claimed her good senses again and to do that she had to return to Manhattan.

"My flight leaves at 8:45 in the morning."

If her other words had not left him speechless, the ones she spoke last, left him panicked according to the way his eyes widened.

"But you just got out of the hospital."

Sophia cocked her head and placed her hand on her hip, giving him a knowing look. From their spirited encounters, he knew good and well that she'd completely recovered from the bout that led her to the hospital.

"Really? Is that your argument?"

He smiled and began pulling out containers of what appeared to be Asian food.

"Did you get Chinese? I thought you had bags of groceries." She walked over to peek inside the bags.

"No, Thai. Do you eat it?" He turned to grab a couple of plates from the stainless steel rack near the pantry. "I have groceries, but I thought I would also grab something we could eat right away."

"I love Thai food, if it's authentic, but not sure how it will do on a stomach that has been taking only liquids for the past couple of days."

"It's as authentic as it gets. I had the owner make you a very bland dish of rice and chicken." Ethan opened all the containers and slid a plate and a small container towards Sophia. "Toey has been in the country for about ten years. She came to live with her older brother who was attending Harvard Law School at the time. Now he is a successful lawyer at a prominent firm in Concord."

He spooned some curry over his rice and watched Sophia as she scooped out two heaping spoons of rice and chicken on her plate. "While Nakul, Toey's brother, studied for long hours, she did all the cooking for him and his study partners. Everyone loved Toey's cooking, so after Nakul went to live in Concord, she brought over their aunt who'd raised them and together they opened Bangkok, their Thai restaurant." He picked up his plate and directed her to the table. "Come on," He pointed his chin towards the table, "let's sit at the table like decent folk."

Sophia put her plate down and walked back to the kitchen.

"What do you want to drink?" She asked him over her shoulder.

"Just grab me a bottle of water from the fridge."

She did and poured herself a glass of sports drink.

"Grab a couple of napkins while you're up." He called to her.

Sophia got the napkins, grabbed the drinks and sat at the table with Ethan. She didn't want to think about how at ease she was moving around his home. She didn't want to think about how their casual familiarity with one another was profoundly intimate. She definitely didn't want to think about how empty her apartment would feel when she arrived tomorrow morning.

So she didn't.

"I take it, the restaurant has been a success."

"No, ma'am. You don't get to make small talk. It's time for the big talk. Don't you think?"

Sophia gave Ethan a crooked smile.

"Well can we eat first?"

"Yes."

So they did. In silence, with both trying to avoid looking at the other.

Because Sophia had gone more than two days with no solid foods, it didn't take long for the rice and chicken to fill her.

"That was delicious." She said as she pushed away the plate still half-filled. "No doubt the restaurant stays busy." She watched him take the last few bites of his food, push his plate away and drink down half of the contents of the water bottle. She tried not to stare at his mouth but it called to her. She bit her bottom lip then quickly looked away when his eyes met hers.

Sophia cleared her throat.

"There is a lot to cover. Where should we start?" She said it as if she was a reporter about to interview him.

Ethan wiped his mouth with the napkin and his expression became steely serious.

"I want to talk about the fact that we didn't use protection."

"Ethan, I—"

He didn't let her finish her statement.

"I want to apologize for behaving so irresponsibly. Trust me. That has never happened before."

She raised a brow.

"Why now, with me?" Her voice was low and cautious.

"I don't know. All I can say is that I've never wanted anyone the way I want you."

She noticed that he didn't use the word "wanted."

"Why now?" She asked again. "That hasn't always been the case."

"It has *always* been the case, baby."

Damn him.

How could one simple word make her tingle and melt all at the same time? Her body may be betraying her, but her mind distinctly remembered all the times he treated her like shit. She frowned in frustration.

Before she could say anything, he reached across the small table and gently squeezed her hand and held it. The air in the room became electrically charged. And as if he knew what the outcome would be if he didn't put some distance between them, he let go of her hand.

"I know you don't believe me, but I hope you will give me the chance to explain." She just stared at him, waiting for him to continue.

"It was not my intention to make love with you without a condom."

Is that what they were doing? Making love? Somehow she'd envisioned making love as being two people who were in love, in bed, in the dark and so forth. She and Ethan fit none of the criteria.

"What?" He asked, puzzled.

"What?" She returned.

"You had a weird look on your face."

"I was just thinking about what you were saying." She didn't lie; she had been thinking about what he was saying, just not the part he was focused on. She wanted to know where he was going with the "no condom" thing and decided not to put him out of his misery just yet.

Ethan felt as if he was getting nowhere.

"Sophia, what I'm trying to say is, if you're pregnant, then we will deal with it together."

Deal with?

She raised a brow.

"Meaning?"

"Meaning, I plan to be a full-time father to our child." His eyes held hers and she knew he meant it.

She looked away and stared at the half-eaten chicken and rice dish.

What would it be like to have a baby with
Ethan? To be in his life forever? A tiny, dark haired,
dark eyed baby, full of spunk, full of life. What would
it be like to hold a baby that belonged to the both of
them and watch he or she grow up?

She would never know.

Ethan watched as the clouds grew dark behind
Sophia's eyes.

"Sophia?" She looked up at him. "I'm sorry I
wasn't more careful."

"A baby is the least of my worries, Ethan."

"If you're worried about my health record, I—"

"That's not what I meant." But then a question
appeared in her eyes.

"Yes, I'm healthy." He assured her.

She chuckled, because he knew what she was
thinking.

"So am I. If I didn't know for sure before, I
definitely know now. They took every test possible. I
thought I would start leaking from all the holes they
poked in me at the hospital."

"That's next on the agenda, but I want to make
sure that you promise to contact me if you're
pregnant."

To Sophia that sounded like he planned for
their relationship or rather their dealings, would be

back to status quo when she left his house in the morning. He must have known what she was thinking because he added, "I'm hoping that I will see you often enough where you won't have to go out of your way to contact me."

Not sure about the prospects of either option, she decided to put him out of his misery.

"I can't have children, Ethan."

It was brief but she saw a tiny bit of sadness flicker across his features. She tried not to read anything into it.

She figured he would cheer with relief, but instead, he held her hand again and as if he knew how devastating it was to her, he squeezed it and held her eyes for the longest time. She felt like he was asking permission to share her pain.

"I'm sorry, Sophia." His words were not condescending or dripping with pity, they were sincere and she knew that he meant them.

The doorbell rang. Perfect timing. She needed a minute to get herself together.

Ethan excused himself and returned shortly carrying a large brown envelope. He placed it on the table.

"You mentioned someone was stalking you."

Sophia glanced at the envelope and then back at Ethan. She didn't have time to dwell on her curiosity because Ethan's face had become hard and unreadable. The change was so drastic, she flinched.

Who was this man? Was he some sort of chameleon? He changed like a lizard playing on a rainbow.

For the next half hour, Ethan listened while Sophia told him about a former client of hers who had become obsessive, to the point that she had to get a restraining order to keep him away from her dance studio. There was no doubt in Ethan's mind that the man had something to do with Sophia's poisoning.

She'd even received a threatening letter from him right before she left for Boston.

"Did you tell the police about the letter?"

"No."

"Why not!" His tone was a little more forceful than he'd intended but just thinking about someone deliberately trying to harm her had him on edge.

"I didn't think it was necessary, Ethan." She looked everywhere but at him. He was sexy as hell when he was angry. Surely she must be going mad. Who gets turned on by someone yelling at them?

Well he wasn't exactly yelling at her. She knew he was upset by the situation. But why? Why did he even care?

Ethan took a deep breath and took a drink of water before he continued.

"Why not? You thought it was important enough to go to the police to keep him away from your studio."

"I didn't know it was from him."

Ethan frowned and looked pointedly at her.

She rolled her eyes.

"I've had to deal with a few jealous wives, reporters trying to get me to give them the scoop on some of my elite clientele, you name it." She took a deep breath. "There's always something. I was looking forward to seeing Candice and Alex so I just brushed it off." She paused and frowned as if remembering something. She sat back in her chair; her voice lowered. "He was there."

"Who was there? Where?"

"Why hadn't I remembered?"

"Remembered what? Sophia!"

"Julius. He was at the airport." She looked towards the window seat in the kitchen. "I was looking out of the airplane window and I could've sworn one of the workers was staring at me. When I looked his way, he turned and walked off." She turned to look at Ethan again. "At the time, I didn't think anything of it. I was beginning to get paranoid and figured I was just imagining it. But now that I think about it, I remember him telling me once that he worked catering for one of the airlines."

His face twisted. "But there's no food service from New York to Boston."

"I know, but it was lunch time and I bought a salad at a kiosk right before I boarded."

Ethan stared at her wide-eyed. "We need to call the police." He was on his feet getting the phone off the wall in his kitchen.

"And tell them what? I'll contact the officer that did the restraining order when I get back to New York tomorrow. How could he have poisoned my salad?"

"There's too much of a coincidence for my comfort, and if you think I'm letting you go back to New York with that maniac on the loose, you have another thing coming, Sweetheart. I don't care if I have to tie you up and gag you."

Eyes wide and dumbfounded she simply sat at the table and stared at him. She should have been pissed by his authoritative tone, but instead found herself wondering if she would be able to check off yet another of her bucket list sexual fantasies.

Chapter 10

Truth Time

"What is it, Dixon? You've been pacing the floor since you got here. Is it Candice's mother? Has she gotten worse?"

Dixon Phoenix smiled at the woman lying on the sofa wrapped in a beautiful handmade quilt.

"I'm here to take care of you, dear friend, not for you to be worried about my family. Now, what can I get you?"

"You can get your behind in a seat. You're driving me crazy walking the floors like you've been doing."

He sat and told her that he'd heard from Landon and though, Mrs. Carwin had suffered a mild stroke, she was doing much better and would be released from the hospital in a day or so.

Over the past two days, Gloria and Dixon had thrown off the formality of employer/employee protocol. He'd taken her home from the hospital when her daughter couldn't make it. He'd made her comfortable on the sofa because her recent surgery did not allow her to climb the stairs in her townhome. He'd made sure she had something to eat and though she protested emphatically, he had not left her in two days.

Dixon figured it was the least he could do. She had taken care of him in more ways than was obvious. She was confidant and always always found the bright side of things, even when it came to his wife Jocelyn, and that was a difficult feat.

Jocelyn had never been kind to Gloria, yet Gloria never spoke ill of her nor did anything untoward when it came to Jocelyn. Every time Jocelyn did something to ruin Dixon's day, Gloria did something to make it ten times better.

Dixon looked at the woman wrapped in her grandmother's quilt and wondered how such a small person could hold a heart as large as hers.

"I know you better than you know yourself, Dixon Phoenix. What's bothering you? You've been in another world since Mr. Powers left here Saturday morning."

Dixon didn't know how much of his meeting he should reveal to her. He knew he could trust her with the information; however he wasn't sure how she would react to it.

Before he could answer, his cell phone rang. It was Jocelyn. He started to ignore it, but knew there was no ignoring Jocelyn.

"This is Dixon." He said flatly.

"Well I hope so, who else would be answering your phone?"

"Hello Jocelyn." Dixon noticed Gloria put her ear buds in her ears and pick up a magazine. He gave her an expression as if saying, you don't have to do that. She pointedly ignored him.

"What?" He asked Jocelyn, missing the last thing she'd said.

"I said, Beatrice said you hadn't been home in two days." Beatrice was the housekeeper that cleaned on the weekends.

"Neither have you. Do you want something in particular, Jocelyn? I know you didn't just call to check on me."

"Where are you?"

"I'm taking care of a sick friend."

There was a pause.

"I need you to fly out here tomorrow. There is a black-tie dinner and everyone is expecting the both of us."

"Didn't you hear me? I said, I'm taking care of a sick friend. And even if I wasn't, I told you I don't want to be involved with anything that has anything to do with Cloudy."

Another pause.

141

"Since when do you take care of sick friends?"

"There are a many number of things that you are unaware of in my life."

Dixon walked over to the bookshelf and ran his finger along the spines of classic novels Gloria had on her shelf, wishing this was not his life.

Jocelyn spoke as if she'd heard nothing he'd said prior.

"There is a flight that arrives at four-thirty. That should give you plenty of time to get changed and escort me to the dinner."

Dixon looked at the phone like it was malfunctioning. He took a deep breath and ran a hand through his hair.

"I said I'm not going." He replied tersely.

"Well if business has you tied up tomorrow, you can meet me at the end of the week for the convention."

Sometimes he wondered how in the hell he'd lasted as long as he did with Jocelyn.

"Our son is getting married at the end of the week. Or had you forgotten?"

"Oh that. Do they really expect us to stay in Baton Rouge at Alexandra's for the entire weekend?"

She hadn't asked if Candice's mother was still in the hospital or how she was doing. He really hadn't expected her to ask or care, but he figured she pretended so much around everyone else, that she could pretend to show at least a modicum of concern about her future in-laws.

"Goodbye, Jocelyn." He disconnected the call.

If it was up to him, she would be nowhere near the wedding.

He slipped the phone back into his pocket.

Gloria tried not to listen to Dixon's conversation. She wanted to respect his privacy, but also, his conversations with Jocelyn always left her feeling torn. She couldn't hear what they were talking about but the look on his face confirmed it was a carbon copy of the talks they've had of late.

She also tried not to notice how handsome he looked in the jeans that he hardly ever wore. Standing in her living room he looked more like a handsome rancher than a powerful CEO. Because she was in charge of his schedule, she knew he stayed pretty active and it showed. He was well put together for a man in his early sixties.

Gloria had to admit, he was well put together for a man of any age. She'd noticed even some of the very young interns admiring him in hushed tones when she accompanied him to meetings throughout the building.

Seductive Pleasures

He was pacing the floor again and she tried not to notice how his wavy salt and pepper hair made the gray flecks in his eyes even more vivid. They were warm and kind—just as he was.

Gloria often wondered how he and Jocelyn ended up together. Not realizing she'd been staring, she noticed he was saying something to her.

She turned the music down and pulled the ear buds from her ears.

"Huh?"

He chuckled, unaccustomed to catching her off her guard and hearing such a casual tone.

"I was really voicing a comment out loud. I don't know how in the hell I ended up with such a bitch." He nearly spit the last word as if he was trying to rid his mouth of it.

"I was just thinking the exact same thing." When she realized she'd muttered her musing aloud her eyes flew open. "I'm sorry, Dixon. That was out of line."

"The hell it was. It's about time we stop skirting around the issue here."

She was confused.

"Come on Gloria. We're better than that. Though you pretend indifferent, you know you can't stand her."

144

Seductive Pleasures

Gloria tried to sit up, which was taking more strength than she had at the moment.

"Don't sit up. I didn't mean to upset you." He moved quickly to the sofa to help her. Dixon propped a pillow against the arm of the sofa and she was able to sit up a bit while still reclining.

It took her a moment to adjust to her new position. He knew she was feeling more than discomfort when she closed her eyes for a few seconds and took in a few deep breaths.

"Are you ok?" He asked, taking a seat on an ottoman near the sofa.

"I'm fine; it just takes a moment to regroup." She saw the concern in his eyes. "Stop worrying. The doctor said I will be good as new in a few days."

His tone became soft and serious. "Glo, are you truly telling me everything?" Dixon was worried that there was more to the surgery than what Gloria was saying. He knew it wasn't any of his business, but he couldn't help but be concerned.

He knew that all of this, meaning him being there, had long since passed the boundaries of a boss and secretary relationship, but he had a strong need to make sure she was ok. He told himself it was because she'd always looked after him well above the call of duty, but he knew that wasn't completely the truth.

Seductive Pleasures

The truth was, he enjoyed being around her. He loved to be in whatever space she occupied. Just to see her smile and laugh made his heart soar. He watched her work tirelessly for him and for many non-profit organizations—organizations that really made a difference to people who needed help.

He tried to make sure she accompanied him on most of his business trips, because she was efficient. She was also a breath of fresh air. There was nothing pretentious about Gloria. She was everything Jocelyn was not.

She answered him, bringing him back to the question he'd asked.

"Yes, Dixon. It was just a biopsy. The doctors didn't see anything to cause them alarm when they went in, but I will know for certain if there is any cancer when I go back for the follow up in a few weeks."

"A few weeks? I will call—"

"You will call no one." She placed her hand on his. "You've done so much and I appreciate it, but I need to deal with this in my own way…in my own time." She tilted her head and gave him an apologetic smile. "Now what issue have we been skirting around?" She asked trying to refocus him.

Dixon refused to think about the possibility of losing her to cancer. He also felt she was in too much pain to have just undergone a simple biopsy, but he wouldn't press her further.

"What do you think of my wife?"

Gloria didn't know how to answer that question, because most times she tried not to think of her at all.

"I don't understand the question."

Dixon smiled.

"You're an intelligent woman, Gloria. What do you think of my wife?"

Gloria closed her eyes and breathed heavily pretending she was asleep.

"That bad, huh?"

She opened her eyes and just stared at him. It was clear she didn't know how to respond.

"I need to go to the bathroom. Will you help me up?"

Dixon knew she was stalling, which was fine, he needed a minute to gather his courage to say what he had to say. He helped her up and watched her walk gingerly to the bathroom near the stairs.

Even in the pale blue pajamas she appeared regal. He closed his eyes and thought about how his life would have been different if Gloria was his wife;

then he thought of his sons and knew he wouldn't trade them for anything, but what, oh what could life have been like with a woman who actually cared about him and things that really mattered. What a formidable team they would have made.

Dixon was sitting on the sofa with his eyes closed when Gloria returned, and as if it was the most natural thing in the world, she sat next to him and leaned her head on his shoulder.

"Do you want to lie down?" He asked softly, enjoying the feel of her next to him.

"No, I'm fine."

"I'm in love with you, Gloria and have been for a very long time."

"Oh?"

That wasn't the reaction he was expecting. Well, actually he didn't really know what he was expecting, because he hadn't expected to blurt it out like that. Nevertheless, he'd said it and there was no taking it back now.

"Yes, and after my son's wedding this weekend I'm filing for divorce. I can't be a part of this farce any longer."

She said nothing.

"I'm sorry for just dumping it all out on you like this but I couldn't go another moment without

148

letting you know how I feel. And whether you want me or not, my marriage has run its course."

"I'm so sorry, Dixon."

"Don't be; I'm not."

She looked up at him. "But you've been together forty years…"

"Forty years too long."

She still had not addressed his feelings for her and she knew that he was waiting.

"It broke my heart to sit back and watch such a good man get emotionally beat down by his own wife." Dixon didn't say anything. "I'm sorry for speaking out of line." She said softly.

He put his arm around her. She did not pull away.

"You didn't say anything that isn't true."

"It's just that she is so…so…so…" She paused for a moment searching for the right words. "Callus." She finally got out. "I wanted you to know that she didn't deserve you. So I went out of my way to make sure you knew it."

"Like the cake."

"Yes. I wanted you to know that I knew you. That I knew what you needed and what you liked." Gloria shook her head. "She didn't deserve you. You are too good."

Her words floated over him as if he were in a dream. How had he lived so long without having her in his arms? Even if she would never let him hold her again, for this moment he was happy—an emotion he only experienced with her and his sons.

"For all I've let her get away with, there isn't much that I deserve. I figured she was my punishment for not being man enough to stand up to her."

"Whatever wrong you've done in your life, you've paid for it. I've seen her in action. You deserve better, Dixon. You deserve to be loved hard and treated like a king."

"From your lips…"

"God hears you." She whispered, her head still resting on his shoulder.

"How can you be so sure?" He squeezed her gently.

"Because I love you, too."

Dixon's heart raced and he prayed to the heavens that he'd heard her say what he thought he heard.

"Say it again." He breathed, barely able to speak.

"Though I wish it was under different circumstances, I love you, Dixon Phoenix."

Dixon gathered Gloria in his arms, careful not to hurt her, and kissed the top of her head—loving the texture of her natural hair against his cheek. He wanted to call the lawyers as soon as possible, wedding or no wedding. Not sure if he could even wait another minute let alone another week to start the process of being free of Jocelyn.

"You know she won't make it easy on you."

Dixon was still reeling from Gloria's confession that it took him a moment to understand what she meant.

"The divorce?"

"Yes. She's going to fight you like a sack of panthers floating down stream."

He looked down at her, scrunched his eyebrows at her unorthodox analogy and shook his head.

"No she won't."

It was her turn to look at him as if he'd grown a second head.

"In what world are you living in?"

He kissed her head again and rubbed her cheek with the back of his hand.

"In the world that I found out yesterday morning that Landon's business partner, Ethan Powers, is the son of Jocelyn Corbett Phoenix."

Chapter 11

Tuesday
Baton Rouge—Together

The large columned white house sat on a hill as if it reigned over the majestic trees that guarded it. The trees seemed to rise and bow, paying the sun homage for its company. They gently swayed in the wind, holding hundreds of years of secrets that were privy to only them. Moss hung like thick nets among the stately giants, adding mystery and intrigue to the landscape that was uniquely Southern Louisiana.

"I feel like I should've brought corsets, hats and gloves." Sophia whispered.

Despite the headache that plagued him since their departure from Boston, Ethan couldn't stop the thought of Sophia in only a corset, hat and gloves from creeping into his mind. He tried to keep his face passive so they would at least make it up to Alex's house before they both ignited. Neither of them could control their passion for each other. It was what finally convinced her to stay in Boston until the trip to Baton Rouge

She'd refused to see reason when it came to her safety. She'd fought him at every turn—hence the headache.

As soon as he found out about the incident at the airport, Ethan called the detective who'd been working with Sophia. It turned out that the man stalking Sophia had not been scheduled to work that day and no one claimed to have seen him. There was nothing the police could do. Ethan had been livid.

He hadn't told Sophia, but he'd launched his own investigation. He would tell her if and when he received information from the private detective he'd hired. Even though their fights usually led to some off the charts sex, he wanted to see what he could find out before he told her.

Ethan wasn't sure why he'd taken such a personal interest in Sophia all of a sudden or why she hadn't just told him to go to hell and gone on about her business.

Well, he knew the latter was because he'd promised that *he* would become her next stalker if she left for New York not knowing if that bastard had anything to do with her being poisoned.

"Ethan?"

"Yes?"

"What were you thinking about? I've been talking to you for about a minute and you haven't heard a word I've said."

"How do you know?"

"What did I say?"

"You said you wanted to wear a corset for me later."

She rolled her eyes and looked out the window. Ethan parked in front of the house and looked around.

"The house is dark. Joshua said he and Alex would be here when I arrived."

Sophia looked at him.

"Do they know we're arriving together?"

"No. I wasn't sure how you would feel about them knowing."

"Well, here we are." She flung her hands out. "Together…What are they going to think about that?" The question in her eyes was replaced with an accusation. "The last time we were in the same room together you treated me like a leper."

"That's not true."

She shot him a look that dared him to deny it.

"As a matter of fact, Ethan, we've talked about a lot of things, but what is this?" She moved her finger to indicate the two of them.

To be honest, he really didn't know what *this* was. All he knew was from the moment he saw her in another man's arms, he wanted her more than he ever had and now he couldn't get enough. So he told her.

"I was mad as hell when I saw that guy in the club holding you on the dance floor. I wanted to hold you like that." His confession was spoken in a low and caring tone. "When I saw how drunk you were, I wanted to be the one to take care of you. Then everything seemed to escalate from there and I was involved." Ethan chuckled and shook his head before speaking again. "That feisty mouth of yours makes me want to pull out all my hair sometimes."

And at that moment a conversation with his mother came back to him.

> *"That's when you know you've picked the right one… She will be the one who challenges you and also the one who will give you the most excitement. She will be the one who hides pieces of herself in tiny crevices of your mind… You will never forget her…She will be the one worth keeping, Ethan."*

Sophia noticed the distant look in Ethan's eyes. "What's wrong?"

Ethan ignored her question while his eyes latched on to her mouth. "And sometimes I just want to devour it…Like now."

He reached over the console of the little sports car, grabbed her by the back of her head, brought her mouth to his and kissed her with fierceness that was beyond his control. His heart raced and his manhood begged to be set free. He couldn't get enough of her and it scared the hell out of him.

He wanted to pull her into his lap and let his hands explore the terrain they'd covered many times over the past few days. He wanted to bury himself in her and get lost in the waves of his cravings. He thought if only he could just envelope her in his arms he would be free to think clearly again, but when Ethan attempted to do so, he found she was restrained by the seatbelt.

He was about to release her when he heard her unsnap of the belt. Giving her a moment to free herself from the restraint, he then pulled her into his lap. Ethan buried his face into her hair and inhaled the sweet scent of flowers that he loved so much.

"Oh Phia, what are you doing to me?" He squeezed her tighter. "I can't breathe without being able to inhale you when I do."

She let out a half moan half sigh as she slowly rocked her head back and forth; always loving the feeling of him nestled in her hair. She also loved when he called her "Phia." No one had ever called her that. Landon called her "Soph," but that was the usual nickname for her. She also loved being completely swallowed up by him. How in the world would she get through the next several days without everyone knowing she had the hots for Ethan Powers?

Somehow they managed to get out of the car and walk up the steps to the door without dissolving into each other. There was an envelope stuck to it with Ethan's name on it, so he opened it. A note and a key was tucked inside.

"Joshua and Alex are in New Orleans checking on the sports bar there and visiting with her partner, Greg. They won't be here until tomorrow and Candice and Landon are in town at her parents." Ethan looked down at Sophia as an iniquitous smile curved his lips. "Looks like it's just you and me." He said with a hint of promise.

He used the key to unlock the door and they walked into a spacious living room.

When Sophia stepped inside she nearly gasped. Alex's childhood home was beautiful and grand. She felt like she was in a modern scene from Gone with the

Wind. For some reason grandeur of this magnitude made her feel uncomfortable.

Though she was financially secure now, her childhood had been anything but. Her mother had done what was necessary to keep food on the table. She'd come home exhausted to the bone from working in the fields. She'd done it all—chopped sugarcane, picked tobacco, coffee beans, cocoa and had even worked in the factory making soap. Doing what she had to do, in order to take care of her 3 children.

Many of her school mates had dropped out of school after their fifteenth birthday to marry, but Sophia's mom refused to give in to social customs and insisted all her children finish school. She wanted them to have more choices than she had. Sophia's brother was married and had a family back home in Venezuela and her younger sister had gone to college in Oregon and ended up marrying a guy from Canada where they now lived. She rarely saw her siblings since the death of their mother several years ago.

Manuel had promised to give her a better life than she had in Maracay.

"Sophia?"

"Yeah?" She asked, taking in the room and all its beautiful furnishings.

"You ok?"

"Beautiful, isn't it?" She whispered.

"Yes." He responded, never taking his eyes away from her.

Sophia turned to look at him and said, "Since no one is here, no one will have to know that we've arrived together."

Ethan tried not to feel disappointed by her not wanting anyone to know they'd arrived together, but failed. He wasn't sure why he felt let down, because it wasn't as if he'd claimed Sophia as his.

Or had he?

He shook off the feeling and walked back to the car to remove their luggage. When they found their way upstairs, they both noticed the doors were labeled with the names of guests who were supposed to stay at the house through the weekend.

When they saw a door that was marked "Dixon and Jocelyn," Sophia looked up at Ethan.

"When are you going to tell Joshua and Landon that you're their brother?" Ethan had told Sophia about his past and about how he'd been so angry with the Phoenix's that he'd vowed to ruin them. He'd also shared with her that after getting to know them, Ethan was sure that no one knew of his existence except for Jocelyn, which is why he'd taken the brown envelope that had been delivered to his home and shared its contents with Dixon Phoenix.

Ethan had not gotten the response he'd expected from Dixon. The man was naturally disturbed by the revelation at first, but then seemed almost...relieved.

"I don't know, but definitely not this weekend."

Sophia nodded her head understanding that Ethan didn't want to ruin Landon and Candice's wedding by presenting himself as an illegitimate Phoenix. He was also a bit apprehensive about what the truth would do to their relationship, business and personal.

"Where's my room?" Sophia asked.

Ethan hadn't found one with his name on it either.

"I don't know. Maybe this is the couple's wing." He grinned and found his way to the other side of the house, and just as he suspected there were three doors. His room was first then there was a door marked, "Chelsea" and Sophia's room was on the end.

"Who's Chelsea?" they both asked at the same time.

They laughed.

"Maybe she is a relative of Candice." He stated.

"Maybe." Sophia agreed.

They both went to their assigned rooms to put away luggage and hang the bags that contained their wedding attire.

Sophia thought it very ironic that Landon asked Ethan to be in the wedding because he'd come to look at him like a brother and it turns out that Ethan is actually his brother. Sophia shook her head and hung the garment bag carrying her bridesmaid dress on the back of the door. She turned and looked at the bed wondering if she would get a chance to sleep in it, then left the room to see what Ethan wanted for dinner.

Chapter 12

...But You.

She turned out to be what Ethan wanted for dinner, so again they found themselves famished in the middle of the night and raiding Alex's fridge. There is just something so profoundly intimate about a man and woman moving around the kitchen together, although wearing next to nothing may have something to do with the feeling as well.

Sophia and Ethan had been together for nearly a week and neither thought it was insanely odd that prior to that, they hadn't so much as had a conversation when they were in the same room. Sophia looked over at Ethan while he was slicing a tomato for their sandwiches and asked the question that had yet to be addressed.

"Why were you so mean to me for all those months?"

Ethan looked up and bathed his eyes in the sight of Sophia standing in the opened refrigerator. There was just something about seeing her standing there wearing only his t-shirt and her panties. It wasn't possessiveness, but a feeling that she somehow was a part of him, warmed his heart. Maybe it was possessiveness.

How could he tell her that by avoiding her, he was avoiding an addiction that could have possibly hindered his plans? In his office the day she was released from the hospital, he'd claimed her with his mouth and every other part of his anatomy that connected with hers.

"I couldn't believe I'd found you again." He unintentionally voiced aloud.

"Again?" She asked closing the refrigerator and walking over to the island in the middle of the kitchen. Like the rest of the cabinetry, it was well crafted with an artistic appeal. The smooth dark counter was in stark contrast to the painted white cabinets.

"I couldn't believe how attractive you were and we seemed to hit it off very well." His statement was efficient enough to distract her from his previous confession.

"That sounds like a good thing to me."

"Much too good." He placed the knife on the counter and leaned against it, facing her. "You have to keep in mind that though I'd invested everything I had in the company Landon and I own jointly, my goal was to destroy the Phoenix name."

"And what does that have to do with treating me like shit?"

"You were an attraction I couldn't afford." Ethan stepped towards Sophia, grabbed her around her waist and pulled her into him. "Like now, I can't seem to not touch you." He brushed his lips across hers and whispered, "I can't seem to not want to kiss you whenever you're near."

Sophia closed her eyes and her bones turned into jelly.

He drew her close, inhaled the flower scent in her hair and could feel pieces of himself floating away, being replaced by everything that was Sophia Ilarraza.

"I was seduced by the very presence of you and I knew that I would have to keep you more than an arm's length away to be able to accomplish my goal."

Sophia snuggled into Ethan's chest.

"Well, I'm not more than an arm's length away now."

"And I don't want you to ever be again."

Sophia become rigid.

He felt it, but said nothing.

She pulled away from him slightly to look up at him.

"That phone call I overheard, that day in your office…"

"Yes? What about it?"

"What was all that about? You said, 'Phoenix doesn't have a leg to stand on' and that something was going to ruin him.'"

"Come, let's sit." Ethan guided Sophia to a chair at the head of the dining table. He sat and gently tugged her waist so she could sit on his lap, but she pulled away and sat in the chair nearest him. He took a deep breath to force down the disappointment.

"The day Candice and Landon had to fly here to check on her mom, Landon asked me to handle the Franklin deal. He'd been working on it a while. Because I was involved in some negotiations with buyers of several of our properties, Phoenix handled Franklin on his own." He saw her eyes searching his. "Some acquaintances of mine had some run-ins with Bruce Franklin before, and I knew how shady he was. He looked squeaky clean on paper but he was a master at duplicity."

Ethan looked away from Sophia, trying to focus on anything but her.

"I had some outside lawyers review the contracts and discovered the holes that were too small for even a skilled lawyer's eyes."

"How could those lawyers see something others couldn't?"

"Because of the acquaintances and their devastating losses, I knew where to look."

"And you kept it from Landon." He nodded his head. "You were going to use the Franklin deal to sabotage Landon?"

Her eyes held his.

"Yes."

She looked away.

"When Landon had to go out of town, it was my perfect opportunity, but…"

She turned back to him. "But what?"

"But you."

"Me?"

"Yes, that was the night I took you home drunk."

"I still don't understand."

"The next morning when I was at the hospital with you, Dixon Phoenix went out of his way to help."

Ethan wanted Sophia to understand why he felt the way he did, that the seed for revenge had been planted from an early age. It had been cultivated from the moment he'd found out what an orphan was and that he, in fact, was one. It grew each time he was moved from one foster home to another.

He told her about his early years as they were told to him. Although he knew now, no one knew at the time, how he'd ended up living with a convent in upstate New York. When the convent could no longer afford the property, the nuns were assigned to parishes along the east coast and the baby who was named Ethan by the nuns was given over to the state.

Ethan was about five when he went to the first foster home. He was treated horribly by the family and the kids at school teased him because he had no *real* mother or father. He told her how he blamed his birth parents for his miserable life.

He lived with two more foster families. The Holcomb's made him feel like a member of the family until Sharon Holcomb, his foster mother, became pregnant with their first child. Taking care of two children was not in their budget, so they claimed.

When he was eight years old and living with his third foster family, he was sent to the school nurse one Friday after fainting in class. The nurse determined he was under nourished and Ethan confessed he was not allowed to eat until after all his chores were done, but because there were always so many, he was never done. He told the nurse that he usually only ate lunch at school.

Janice Powers was the school nurse who refused to let him return to the foster family. Because of her job, she was witness to more horror afflicted on children that she cared to count, but for some reason Ethan immediately captured her heart. She was good friends with the social worker who was in charge of his case so she was able to talk her into letting Ethan go home with her that night. She fed him and gave him a comfortable and safe place to sleep. He stayed the entire weekend and when Monday rolled around, Janice fought like hell to keep him forever.

She won.

It was the first time anyone had ever fought to keep him.

Sophia understood how a child would need someone to blame for his miserable childhood. She also knew the memory of it all was possibly still quite painful. She recognized all too well how pain buries itself into a person's being and drains them like a tick.

"My mom was worried about me. I was angry for a very long time; so she began looking for my birth parents, hoping to give me closure."

"I take it she found them."

"She found out who my mother was, but it wasn't until years later that I knew the whole truth."

"I take it that you never contacted her."

"No." He didn't elaborate further and she didn't push him to.

"How did Mr. Phoenix take it when you told him everything?"

"Not as I expected."

Sophia didn't ask anything else about the meeting. She figured if he wanted her to know, he would tell her. All this talk was forcing him to revisit past hurts and she didn't want to be the cause of having him endure any more than he had to. Yet, she did want to know what prompted him to let go of his animosity.

"So what happened with Bruce Franklin?"

"He and his lawyers were so complacent about their underhanded business tactics that when my lawyers presented the signed contracts, they were so eager to close the deal, they didn't bother to read the new fine print."

"You changed the original contracts?"

And with a smile that she could have licked from corner to corner, he nodded his head.

The deal will ruin him.

"When you heard me on the phone, I was making the changes to ruin Franklin, not Landon. With the contracts as they were, Landon wouldn't have had a leg to stand on with the other property deals."

She was beginning to understand and to her surprise, her heart felt lighter. She hadn't realized that subconsciously she was feeling guilty about whatever was going on between them. Every time she'd lost herself in him, she'd felt a prick of betrayal towards Landon and his family.

"So, Dixon helping me out at the hospital made you change your mind about something you'd harbored all your life?" She asked with a hint of skepticism.

"That… and I began to think about how the family had treated me since Landon and I became partners."

She understood. She'd seen Ethan, Joshua and Landon together and he'd gotten along with them like they'd been friends for years.

"Initially, when Dixon wouldn't give Global Green to us without the condition that Landon had controlling interest, I figured the Phoenix's were just as I'd imagined them being."

"And how was that?"

"Controlling. Using their money to make everyone pawns in their game or seemingly inferior to them."

"And now?"

"Now I realize that Dixon was just looking out for his son, not because of who he is, but because he's…his son." He looked away for a long moment.

"Besides my mother, they are the only people who have taken me in and treated me like family."

"Ironic isn't it?"

"Very."

"And Jocelyn?" She questioned.

"Jocelyn is a whole other animal." He responded. "She hasn't been around much, but when she is, the temperature drops twenty degrees." He frowned. "The first thing she wanted to know was who my family is and it took everything I had not spit out, *you*."

"Yea, she doesn't like me much. First, my accent must indicate to her that I'm not very smart, because she tends to talk slow to me and explain even the simplest things."

Ethan chuckled softly.

"And secondly, being a dancer is akin to being a whore in her book…I can tell by the way she avoids touching me—even with her eyes."

"The woman who birthed me is a piece of work, indeed."

Sophia didn't know why she did it, but she got up and sat in his lap. His arms snaked around her and sweet anticipation of something delicious drummed inside her.

171

"One more question…" She stated, trying to focus on anything but the way he felt against her.

"Yes?"

"You never said how I was the cause of you not pushing the deal through as you originally intended."

"I'd been avoiding you, because you were friends with the family and I knew that if we got involved then there was a chance you could get hurt—or even worse."

"Even worse?"

"That you would think I'd used you to get to them."

"Oh."

"I couldn't stand the thought of you thinking badly of me."

"But, why the change? You could've kept avoiding me."

"I couldn't."

"Why?"

"I wanted you."

"And?"

"You don't understand. I wanted *you*—no other."

She looked up at him, trying not to be captured in the dark pools of his eyes.

"And now?" She managed to ask.

"I don't think I will ever tire of wanting you."

"Oh."

He swallowed her word in a kiss and proceeded to show her just how much he wanted her.

Ethan watched Sophia pour them both another glass of tea. It was 3:00am, but they'd finally managed to eat. Sophia placed the glass on the table in front of him and her cheeks darkened when she thought about what they'd done on that table—in someone else's house. It embarrassed her to think of how little control she had around Ethan.

She'd scrubbed the table mercilessly. And even now her eyes kept darting to the edge where she'd shamelessly given herself to him.

"It won't tell on you; I promise."

Sophia looked up at Ethan, his face masked in quiet humor.

"Oh shut up."

She stood and walked over to the radio on the kitchen counter and switched it on. A sultry R&B tune flowed into the room. She closed her eyes and swung her hips and shoulders from side to side.

Sophia was startled by a hand at her waist. Ethan turned her to face him.

"Dance with me, Baby."

173

She smiled and lifted her brows in surprise. He pulled her close and something in her soul stirred.

If this man can dance, I'm done for.

He looked down at her expectantly and she realized he was serious. So she placed her hand in his and he held her with hands so painstakingly sure that Sophia couldn't help the beam of delight that spread across her face as her body pressed into him.

The music swam around them and she waited for the rhythm to take hold. The slow da dum da dum begged her hips to move; she wanted to rock them into him, but decided to focus on the confidence in which he held her.

Why was she nervous? They'd done all sorts of sensual things over the past few days so she couldn't fathom why little butterflies were taking flight in her belly. But for some reason, being held in the kitchen of Scarlet O'Hara's home, seemed infinitely more intimate than their love making.

Dancing was her passion. She just happened to make a living being able to do it. Even though she taught dance and had taken this position with countless men, somehow this was different. She didn't know how or why. It just was.

So Ethan Powers hadn't simply asked her to dance, to Sophia, he was asking her for peek inside the parts of her soul where her passion was guarded and kept safe. He was asking her to share it with him.

His hand shifted a little lower on her back and he pulled her into him. Sophia closed her eyes and breathed in the moment.

The start set the tone for the entire dance, and she knew that if he didn't get it just right she would unconsciously find him a tad lacking—she breathed and waited. The beat caught hold and with the ease of a swan in flight, he followed it and took her along for the ride. In bare feet over the beautifully polished floors, Ethan glided her through the kitchen and into the living room.

Dear Lord...She exhaled silently.
The man can dance.

Sophia silently prayed for the strength she knew she would need.

Chapter 13

Where Is Kristina?

"I don't understand. Where's Kristina?" Sophia asked in a whispered tone. She looked at Ethan who was sleeping next to her, clearly undisturbed by the recent ringing of her cell phone.

Sophia climbed out of bed and threw on Ethan's t-shirt dragging her eyes along his bare chest before she tipped out of the room.

"Kristina didn't show up last night." The woman replied.

"What do you mean—didn't show up? She knew I would be out of town and agreed to take my classes."

"No one has been able to get in touch with her since we left the studio, Saturday night."

This was so unlike Kristina that Sophia immediately suspected something was wrong.

She walked into the room down the hall from Ethan's and opened her suitcase lying on the bed. Sliding on a pair of leggings, she asked Erica, her part-time office assistant what happened when clients began to show for their lessons.

"I did the class." Erica replied a little hesitantly.

"You did." She stated, more surprised than accusingly.

"Yes."

Erica had only been working for the studio for a few weeks and Sophia had no idea she even knew how to dance. She'd been desperate at the time to find someone to organize all the paperwork and set appointments after the previous girl suddenly quit and ran off to LA with one of the guys she'd met at the studio.

He'd come to New York from Kansas to work on Broadway. After a few shows that fizzled off off Broadway, he thought he would try television instead and headed to Hollywood.

Erica had come in at a time when Sophia was elbow deep in paperwork and had no time to sit at the desk to take appointments. After looking at her resume and seeing she'd had several years of experience as an office assistant, Sophia hired her immediately.

She'd turned out to be a wiz in the office and very pleasant on the phone with the clients. Sophia was pleased with Erica's work ethic and performance, now it seems that she had even more reason to be thankful for hiring her.

"You're a dancer?"

"Not anymore." The words were spoken so softly that Sophia was sure there was a story behind them, but she couldn't give it her attention right now. Her main concern was Kristina.

"Thank you Erica."

There was a pause

"I hope you aren't upset, but I didn't know what else to do. No one complained…It actually went very well."

"From what I know about you so far, I'm sure it went better than 'very well.'" Sophia sighed. "I'm just worried about Kristina. This is so unlike her."

"I thought she was here when I arrived yesterday, because her car is still here."

"It is?" Uneasiness began to form a knot in Sophia's stomach.

"Yea, but she leaves it all the time when she spends the night with Daniel."

Kristina's boyfriend, Daniel, worked and lived near the dance studio and often picked her up when they stayed at his place.

Keeping her voice as even as she could Sophia told Erica to transfer the office calls to the office cell, lock the studio and leave.

"I have a few things to work on before I lock up, but… sure. Everything ok?"

"Lock up now, there is nothing pressing. Please advise the clients that the studio is closed for the next two weeks."

"What's going on?" Erica asked, concern lining her words.

"I'm not sure Erica, but to be on the safe side, I don't want you there. Consider it a paid vacation." She could tell Erica was still confused but she agreed.

"Call me when you leave the office. In the meantime I will see what I can find out about Kristina."

"Ok… but—"

"But what? Don't you know how to take a vacation?" She was trying to lighten the mood.

"Are you firing me?"

Sophia sat on the bed and rubbed the center of her forehead. *Shit!* She thought. She'd just remembered Erica had a lot of work on her desk. They'd received the contracts from Helix Studios. The production company who'd contracted Sophia to do the choreography for an upcoming movie.

Sophia knew that no matter what she said, Erica would be in the office at all times of the night working to get all the paperwork done.

179

"Damnit, I forgot about Helix." She thought a moment. "On second thought, I need you to bring the contracts out to me in Baton Rouge…Can you be here this evening?"

"Sure!" Relief and eagerness exploded with the single word.

"Fine. I will text you the details."

Flying her to Baton Rouge was the only way she knew to keep her safe, because her gut told her that something terrible had happened to Kristina. Sophia knew for certain that Kristina was not with Daniel. Kristina recently found out that Daniel had a wife in the suburbs while he'd been taking her to his apartment in the city.

As soon as Erica disconnected the call, Sophia called the detective who was working her stalking case.

Ethan reached for his phone on the night stand—10:26am. He never slept that late. Replacing the phone, he smiled and remembered that he hadn't slept too much; he just hadn't gotten to sleep until right before dawn.

He turned over to pull her close and found she was not there. The bed suddenly felt deserted and cold.

It was the first time he'd woken up without her since the day after she'd been released from the hospital.

The magnitude of his need for her slammed against his chest. It still shamed him a bit that his desire had prevented her from recuperating as she should have after being hospitalized. Then he remembered that she'd wanted him just as much.

In all his years of life, Ethan could only remember wanting one other thing as much as he wanted Sophia.

A family.

As he pulled the pillow against his chest and her scent filled him, Ethan's heart exploded with the realization that he didn't just want her physically, he wanted her to be *his*.

He wanted her to be his family—his reason.

With that private confession, Ethan realized that whether Jocelyn Phoenix ever acknowledged the fact that he was the son she gave up or not, it didn't matter. Janice Powers was his mother. She'd loved him and shaped him to be the man he is today.

To seek revenge on the Phoenix's would discredit his mother's love. Revenge would state that his mother's love was not enough and he refused to dishonor her that way.

Seductive Pleasures

Ethan sat on the edge of the bed feeling light and hopeful. He'd been driven by darkness for so long, which he was sure didn't have positive outcomes, however this morning he was driven to seek out and capture the heart of a woman whom had no idea that she already held his.

Sophia sat on the porch off of the kitchen and admired the scenery. The grass was green and lush even though it was only early spring. She loved that she didn't need a jacket and enjoyed the feel of the warm breeze on her arms and the sweet smell of the azaleas blooming everywhere. She had an urge to slip off her shoes and let her feet feel the carpet of grass between her toes, but suppressed it when she heard a car door and then voices near the front entrance of the house.

Ethan stepped into the long hallway and heard sounds of conversations drifting up the stairs. Joshua and Alexandra must have made it in from New Orleans.

"Hello." He called out to the three of them as he walked into the kitchen, his eyes lingering on Sophia long enough to let her know she'd been missed but not long enough that anyone else seemed to notice.

Joshua stood up and threw his arm around Ethan.

"Hey, Man. Sorry we weren't here when you got here." He looked over at Sophia. "Sophia says the two of you arrived the same day."

"Yes." He said, looking at Sophia with an unreadable smile. He wondered how much she'd shared with them.

Ethan bent down and gave a seated Alexandra a hug and kiss on her cheek.

"Alex, this is a beautiful home. I can't imagine growing up in such a remarkable place."

"Thanks, Ethan. But it was just home to me." She smiled and waved her arm slowly around the room. "Make yourself at home." She looked at Sophia "You too, Soph."

Ethan looked across the table at Sophia.

"Have you been up a while Sophia?"

"A little while. I've had a few business phone calls to make."

Alex and Joshua looked from Ethan to Sophia then at each other. Alex raised a brow, but said nothing.

"Is everything ok?" Ethan asked Sophia.

"Yes." She said and turned to Alex. "By the way Alex, is there a hotel near here? My assistant will

183

be coming in town this afternoon to bring some contracts we need to go over."

Ethan frowned, because the assistant coming in town was news to him. She hadn't mentioned it before and in fact, had said that everything at work was taken care of so she could be gone at least a week or more if needed. He immediately knew there was something she wasn't saying.

"Your assistant is coming *here*?" Ethan asked with a finger pointing at the table, before Alex had a chance to respond.

All eyes turned to Ethan. It was commonly known that Ethan actively avoided Sophia, so to hear him ask her a direct question *and* with such concern was rather…intriguing—at least it was to Joshua and Alex.

Ethan ignored the surprise gazes from the other two; he focused on Sophia.

"Yes." She said and looked away.

"What aren't you telling me?"

Again Joshua and Alex exchanged a look with raised brows.

"I don't know what you mean." She turned to Alex again, waiting for an answer.

Alex looked from Sophia to Ethan before she realized Sophia was waiting on an answer to her question.

"Ummm…the closest hotel is about seven miles from here. But—"

Sophia's phone rang and she held up a finger to Alex and excused herself from the table.

"Yes this is Sophia Ilarraza…" they all heard her say before she walked out on the porch.

Ethan vaguely heard Joshua ask him a question because he was focused on Sophia's face.

"What do you think Ethan?" Joshua questioned.

"Huh?" Ethan tore his eyes from Sophia to look at Joshua. "I'm sorry. What'd you say, Josh?"

"We were thinking about hitting the links in the morning while the ladies are off doing their foo foo stuff for the wedding. Are you up for it?"

Ethan smiled and looked towards the French doors that led out to the patio where Sophia was still on the phone. Just as he was about to turn back to Joshua to answer the question, he saw Sophia double over as if she'd been struck in the abdomen and her free hand cover her mouth.

Ethan was on his feet and to the door, leaving behind very confused looks on Joshua and Alexandra's faces.

"Phia?" He asked holding her by the shoulders. "What is it?"

She still had the phone to her ear and hand to her mouth shaking her head.

"What is it, Baby?"

The patio door was still open so their conversation was not lost on the couple in the kitchen. However, they were so stunned they had yet to react.

Sophia finally managed to speak.

"It's Kristina."

Ethan knew Kristina was the dancer who worked with Sophia.

"What about her, Babe?"

Sophia collapsed into sobs onto Ethan's chest. He took the phone from her.

"Hello?" He spoke into the phone.

It was Detective Davis. He restated what he'd told Sophia.

Kristina had been found in an alley near the studio, badly beaten and suffering from massive internal hemorrhaging. She was in ICU and had only just become conscious that morning after extensive surgery, still barely able to tell the doctors her name. They had no idea who'd attacked her.

It didn't take the other two long to rush outside when they saw the grief stricken Sophia, though it was apparent that Ethan was not going to surrender her to anyone.

He sat with her on the swing, held her tightly and kissed the top of her head. Alex reached for Joshua's hand and quietly walked back into the house giving them some privacy—knowing there would be time for questions later.

Alex wondered what had transpired to bring the two together, but she knew no matter what it was or if they even knew it yet, they were in love.

Chapter 14

Ghost in My Dreams

"What do you need?" Ethan asked gently, still holding Sophia on the swing.

She'd stopped crying and stared out at the lawn at nothing in particular while she crooned a tuneless hum. He wondered if she was trying to drown out the words of Det. Davis.

Ethan kissed the top of her head. She gave him a weak smile and closed her eyes. He didn't think she was going to answer him, but after a long sigh, she spoke.

"Just this." The playful songs of birds overhead filled the silence on the porch. "Thank you."

He had no idea why she was thanking him, but he didn't voice it. He held her tighter.

"None needed."

Ethan was torn between comforting Sophia and wanting to jump on the first thing smoking to New York. He wanted to find the person who'd attacked Kristina and show him what it felt like to be a victim.

His gut told him that the attack had something to do with Sophia. Just thinking about the possibility of someone wanting to cause her harm, made fear and fury stack up inside of him until he nearly choked. He hoped the detective agency he hired would soon have answers. They were the best in the business and yet had come up with nothing. That frightened him the most, because it meant the person after Sophia was no lovesick fan; he was a sick bastard who was also thorough and skilled enough to have gone undetected.

Unfortunately, he had not gotten the chance to question Det. Davis thoroughly or find out if the police suspected the attack linked to the man Julius, who was stalking Sophia. He also wasn't sure if Det. Davis called Sophia because Kristina worked for her or if he knew something more.

Ethan knew how stubborn Sophia could be and hoped she wouldn't want to go back to New York to be with Kristina. That was a fight she would definitely lose, even if he had to tie her to a chair.

"I'm smart enough to know that this whole thing may have something to do with me."

"None of this is your fault."

She sighed, shifted a little to look at him.

"Yea, I keep telling myself that, but—"

"But nothing." He said, with a gentle but firm tone. "*None* of this is your fault."

Her big round eyes were so vulnerable. He held them with his own and silently promised to keep her safe. He wanted to always be the one to hold her when she was upset; he wanted to be the first to receive her smile at the beginning of each day. Even with everything around them seemingly in turmoil, sitting on the porch holding Sophia, he finally felt at peace. Nothing else mattered but this moment.

Sophia noticed a change in Ethan; the clouds passed from his eyes and she could see him for the first time. For the first time there was no mask to shield him. She could see the little boy who longed for a family. She could see the son who loved his mother. She could see the man who conquered his dreams— she could see Ethan Powers, the man with whom she was falling in love.

The realization that she was in love with Ethan was frightening. Even though his eyes told her he was sincere about wanting to protect her from harm, there still was the ugly little voice that kept whispering reminders of how he'd treated her over the past year.

Sophia placed a hand behind Ethan's neck and lifted a bit to give him a gentle kiss on his lips before easing herself from his lap. He scooted over to give her more room. She wanted to talk to him about something but felt too vulnerable lying in his lap for what she wanted to discuss and yet, when she moved away she felt too disconnected from him. So she put her back against the arm of the large swing and rested her legs on his lap.

Was that a flash a relief she saw in his eyes?

"So, what's going on here?" She moved her finger back and forth between the two of them and then linked her fingers in her lap. "We can't keep our hands off of each other and here lately you're always there when I'm recovering from something horrible."

Her eyes rested on her hands. Even to her own ears, her voice was a mixture of innocence and gratitude. She looked up at him again and couldn't help the slow smile. "And last night...last night you danced with me." Ethan placed his hand on hers. "What does that all mean? And what will it mean after the wedding, when we go our separate ways."

"I'm in love with you, Sophia." His gaze was so intense and his words stated so matter-a-factly that she felt he thought there was no more to be said. On the contrary, she couldn't have heard him correctly. She unconsciously began to draw her knees into her chest, like she did so often when she had a lot on her mind.

Ethan frowned.

"Where're you going?"

She straightened her legs again, though now his hands felt hot through the thin cotton of her skirt. She felt a line of sweat run down her back. The last man she'd allowed to love her and who she loved with every fiber of her being, had killed a piece of her soul. She'd promised herself to never let it happen again. Never.

But Ethan is not Manuel. A little voice echoed in her head.

I'm in love with you, Sophia.

She heard the words over and over as she stared at him, trying to will her voice to work again.

"Say something." He said.

"You've made it a little difficult."

"Not what you were expecting me to say?"

"No." The word was barely audible.

"Then what?"

"I…uh…I thought you would say you wanted us to see each other again…" She searched for the correct words. "Be lovers or something like that."

"I do want us to be lovers."

She said nothing.

"Sophia?"

"But you said…"

"I'm in love with you." He cut her off.

"But you've hated me for so long." She tried to find a way around or through the subject without confirmation from him.

"Haven't you been listening to me the past few days?" He wanted to pull her into his lap but gave her the space she was trying to put between them.

"How could you possibly be in love with me? You barely know me."

"Sophia Ilarraza, you've haunted my dreams for the past two years. For the longest time I thought I was infatuated with a figment of my imagination and then one day there you were, banging your car door into mine."

She frowned. Confused.

"That was a year ago."

"Yes, but I'd already been dreaming and thinking about you for an entire year." His voice drummed beneath the layers of her barrier.
"When I found out you were a friend of someone I was supposed to hate, I had to completely cut you off. I knew that I couldn't go through with my plans and risk hurting you in the process."

Sophia removed her legs from his lap and gathered them beneath her.

"I still don't understand. How had you been dreaming of me for a year and we'd only just met?"

He looked at her for a few moments and she wondered if he would answer her or even if he had an answer.

"The day I buried my mother was one of the most difficult days of my life." He looked away as if the memory was still too difficult to relive. She wanted to reach over and comfort him, but didn't move. "It was a pain I had to bear alone…" He closed his eyes and didn't speak for a long time. Sophia held her breath, feeling his pain while the unshed tears stung her eyes.

"When I could finally force my body to move, I stood and walked away from her. Before I reached my car I heard the sounds of grief that was not unfamiliar to my own." She watched him intently. "I don't know if I was drawn to the sound because I understood the grief or if I didn't want to be alone in mine. At any rate, I walked over to the form I saw crumpled over a grave where a young woman was so consumed with grief that my approach was not noticed."

Sophia stiffened.

"For a moment she let me hold her and offer a modicum of solace."

"Dios!" She exclaimed in a whisper.

"And before I could say anything, she was gone. But I couldn't get the image of her out of my mind nor could I forget how great her grief had been."

With words filled with awe she stated, "I thought I'd dreamed that."

He gave her a soft knowing smile.

"Me too…and then you were there. Standing in the parking lot like a ghost come to life."

Sophia remembered the way Ethan had looked at her that day, like he knew her.

"You were the guy who held me and let me cry in his arms?"

"Yes."

Sophia's mind whirled. She remembered the day well. A tear slid down her face. Ethan said nothing, though he scooted towards her and pulled her into his lap to hold her, trying again to absorb the grief she held on to so tightly.

"I prayed that day." She took a deep breath and wiped away some of the wetness on her face. "I prayed and asked God to help me bear the pain…and then I felt a comforting presence. The next thing I knew I was in the arms of a stranger—you."

"Who was Sparrow?" He asked.

Chapter 15

The Shoes

Gloria opened the front door of her townhouse and was surprised to see Dixon standing there. She tugged on the t-shirt dress.

"Dixon?"

"Last I checked." He said looking down at himself and patting his chest.

Her eyes drank him in, though he wondered if she realized it. After talking with his lawyer all day and contemplating Jocelyn and his son's reaction to the divorce, Dixon needed something good. When he left the office he didn't have a destination in mind, but somehow he'd ended up at Gloria's.

She tugged on the t-shirt dress again, but the action didn't do much to cover her gorgeous pair of thighs. The results of her religious-like workout sessions and clean eating were evident.

Gloria stepped to the side to let him in.

"Whatcha got there?" Indicating the box he held.

Vaguely aware that she'd asked him something, Dixon managed to tear his eyes away from her legs to respond to the question.

"It…it was sitting next to your door." He lifted it to give to her. "Expecting a delivery?"

"I'm always expecting a delivery."

He smiled at her, loving the way her eyes shone with either anticipation or excitement, maybe both. Whatever it was, he didn't care because she was no longer paying any attention to the length of her dress.

Dixon hated to compare the two; nevertheless he couldn't help contrasting Gloria's carefree enthusiasm to Jocelyn's frigid expectancy. Never had Jocelyn just *threw on* something to lounge around the house.

When had *he*?

He was so tired of fitting into a mold someone else created for him. He was tired of schedules, stuffy functions and being around people whom he couldn't stand. He was ready for a change. He was ready for a new life.

"Are you keeping it for ransom?" Gloria asked, trying to tug the box from Dixon's grip.

"Huh?"

She cocked her head to the side and raised a brow.

"Huh?" She mimicked. "You sound like a kid."

Dixon noticed she was trying to get the box. He looked at her mouth and had an overwhelming urge to kiss it.

What was wrong with him? He felt like he did in high school when Becky Sherman showed him her boobs that time she wanted him to write a paper for him. He'd been a brainiac freshman and she was a varsity cheerleader with everything that entailed.

She made an A on the paper.

He followed her around for weeks until her boyfriend told him to back off and his mom grounded him for making a C on his physics project. He'd been so preoccupied with Becky *and her boobs* that his grades began to suffer.

Now, he found himself obsessing over Gloria. He missed her at work and found himself working from home just so he wouldn't see her empty desk. He was starting to lose the taste for a lot of things. He'd actually been contemplating turning over the reins of his corporation to Landon, since he was the only one interested in corporate work. Joshua was content with his early retirement, his yacht and his wife—not necessarily in that order.

Dixon couldn't blame Joshua. He too was ready to…live…to breathe. He also wanted something he'd never had with Jocelyn—passion.

"Dixon Phoenix, if you don't let go of my shoes, I will tackle you to the ground."

Tackled to the ground?

By Gloria?

Wearing that slip of a dress?

My Lord.

Dixon felt a specific part of him spring to life—an action he'd long since forgotten.

He released the box and walked towards the window overlooking her garden. He didn't know whether to feel embarrassed or elated. In the background he heard her opening the box and searched his mind for something... anything, to say to get his *parts* back to normal. That, too, was disturbing.

"Did you say you had a problem?" He wanted to face her but couldn't at the moment. Hiding an erection was something he hadn't done in decades.

"Yes. I have a bit of an obsession with shoes."

A frown displayed his confusion as he turned towards her, forgetting momentarily about his current predicament.

"Shoes?"

"Yes! Aren't these gorgeous?" Gloria extended her leg as she gazed at the shoe on her left foot.

If he spent every last dime of his nearly billion dollar empire buying shoes like the one she wore, it would be worth every damn cent. Who knew shoes could be so sexy?

Is it the shoe or the woman?

He was pretty positive it was the woman but that damn shoe was sexy as sin. Or it could've been the way her dress just barely covered her curvy behind as she extended her leg to get a good look at how high the thin straps circled above her ankle.

Where did she wear those shoes? Definitely not to work. At work, her feet were donned in sensible pumps or boots in the winter, stylish, but nothing like the erection producing sex stilts she wore at that very moment.

And she thought *she* had a problem. He was having a bit of a problem as well, because all he kept thinking about was making love to her while she was wearing those shoes.

It was the sort of shoe women kept on during sex—not trashy at all, but rather ultra sexy. They were definitely the kind that made men and women take notice. Dixon was sure he'd never thought of shoes and sex at the same time and definitely had never ventured to think about the novelty of being seduced by a woman's wardrobe in the bedroom. His life suddenly appeared as bland as communion wafers and he had no one to blame but himself.

The heels were at least five inches.

"I normally don't go for heels this high but the one inch platform at the front takes away an inch." She said, cutting into his thoughts. "Allowing me to walk without falling on my face."

Gloria in stilettos was like seeing a unicorn for the first time—unbelievable, but glad for the revelation because it gives you hope of other impossible possibilities—if that made any sense.

She still hadn't looked at him, still enraptured by the shoe.

"Do you like them?" When after several moments he still hadn't answered, she finally looked up. "Dixon?"

He shifted from one foot to another.

"Yes..." The word was lodged in his throat before it traveled across his dry tongue. He cleared his throat and began again. "Yes, they're lovely."

If someone put a gun to his head, he wouldn't be able to describe any one of Jocelyn's footwear, but this shoe would be ingrained in his mind for a long time. He wouldn't be able to forget her expression when she looked at it.

There were so many things he wanted to say, but he hadn't yet figured out why he'd shown up at her door unannounced.

She seemed satisfied with his answer, looked at the shoe at the end of her outstretched leg and started to take the tissue from its sister still in the box. The soft crunch of the paper reminded him of the sound his foot made on his frozen lawn right before a big snow storm.

He hated winter. There were too many days stuck inside with Jocelyn. Winter was usually when he put in long hours at work.

When they divorced, maybe he would tell them all to go to hell and move to Florida or somewhere in the Carolinas, buy him a modest house on the beach and a little sailboat. He used to love to sail.

When Dixon became too busy with his growing business, he was glad his brother, Cortland, had taught both Landon and Joshua to sail.

Cortland.

He and his brother had never been very close, but he'd loved him dearly. Cortland made his own path and cared very much about championing the causes of those who couldn't take on the task themselves. He bucked all the rules and Dixon was envious as hell. Because Cortland was the son who didn't conform to their family's social customs, Dixon felt obligated to be the "good" son.

He still felt the loss of his brother and regret that they weren't closer. However, Dixon was glad that his own sons were close.

"They are even hotter in person than they were online. I was wondering if the teal would be a true teal. The black and white braid in the back is gorgeous." Gloria was standing and looking down at her feet. She looked up at Dixon. "What?" She asked frowning matching his features.

He shook his head. "I need to go." He blurted, yet, he didn't move.

"Huh? You just got here." It seemed to occur to her then, that she had no idea why. "Is there something you needed or were you just stopping by?"

He simply stared at her. He didn't know why he was there.

"Dixon?"

"I don't know why I'm here." He replied honestly. He turned towards the window again, not looking at anything in particular. "I needed to see you," he breathed, "but I can't talk to you while you're wearing that."

"What?"

Before either could respond, the doorbell rang. Gloria's frown deepened. "Who could that be?"

"What a cliché."

Dixon spun around at the sound of Jocelyn's voice. There she was standing at the door in a somber black pantsuit, her black hair pulled back in a bun in stark contrast to her pale, nearly white face. There was hardly a hint of her African American heritage in her appearance and Dixon knew that's exactly how she preferred it.

"What the hell are you doing her, Jocelyn?" He asked.

Ignoring him for the moment Jocelyn took in Gloria's appearance. She raked her eyes from the stilettos, pausing briefly at the t-shirt dress and certainly not disguising her aversion of Gloria's seemingly untamed locks atop her head. Dismissing her as if she had the right to do so, Jocelyn turned towards Dixon and stepped through the open door as if she'd been invited in.

"What is this?" She asked, walking towards Dixon holding documents in her hand.

"You're a smart woman. What do you think it is?" He hadn't waited until after the wedding. He couldn't wait another moment to get away from her once he had the ammunition to do so.

"If you're having a mid-life crises, Dixon, go on with it, get through it and let's forget about it."

He just stared at her, again, wishing his life had taken a different path.

"I'm not having a mid-life crisis, Jocelyn. I'm having an awakening." Then it occurred to him that Jocelyn was here in Gloria's home. "How did you know I was here?"

"I had you and your little tart here, followed." She waved a hand at Gloria absently, as if there was nothing wrong with having them followed.

Anger sparked inside of him like a fuse at the end of a stick of dynamite.

"How the hell...How the hell..." Each time he sputtered the phrase his voice grew louder. "How the hell did I stay married to you for so long!" His voice exploded.

"Calm down, Dixon. You're not the only man who's slept with their secretary. Though I admit, it is a bit of a cliché."

"What?" Both Dixon and Gloria exclaimed.

"I know you spent the night here the other night." She stated.

"I'm so sorry." Dixon stated in apology.

"All men go through it, Dixon, but we keep it in the family. Not broadcast our troubles by getting a divorce." Her smile was patronizing.

"I wasn't talking to you." Dixon looked at Gloria. "I'm sorry I got you involved in all of this." He turned back to Jocelyn. "For your information, Jocelyn, Gloria has nothing to do with why I want to leave you." He walked to the door. "We are not having this conversation right now and I don't know who the hell you think you are by barging in someone's home like you own the damn place?"

"You're my husband."

"Not for long."

"You can't be serious, Dixon."

"Very."

Dixon turned to Gloria, still standing near the door in her new heels and the short dress. He could only just imagine what Jocelyn thought. He didn't care what she thought about him, but he didn't want his wife to think Gloria was any type of leverage she could use against him. She simply had none.

"I'm so sorry, Gloria. I didn't mean for you to get dragged into my personal affairs."

Gloria nodded and watched Dixon grab Jocelyn by the elbow and herd her out the door.

Dixon walked Jocelyn over to her car.

"I'm leaving you, Jocelyn."

"For that afrocentric tramp in there?"

"Because I have had enough of being in this fraud of a marriage and because I can't stand being around you, and Gloria is not a tramp!" He was livid, but there was no sense in explaining that she was so far out of Gloria's league that the two women may as well live on different planets.

She just stared at him.

"Come on, it's getting late and Kyle and Mavis are coming over tonight to talk about the cruise."

It infuriated him when she did that.

"Are you daft? Did you not just understand what I said?"

"You'll feel better after we've taken a little vacation and you've relaxed a while."

He stared at her in utter disbelief.

"You can even keep your mistress." She patted him on the chest. "Just be discrete, Dixon."

Frustration nearly paralyzed him.

He spoke through gritted teeth.

"Gloria is not my mistress. She is my secretary and my friend. I spent the night here the other night, because she was just home from the hospital and her kid couldn't come to stay with her." He took a deep breath. "Not that I owe you any explanation. You are never home and I don't question it."

"Because you know where I am."

"Half the time, I have no idea where you are and frankly, I don't question you because I don't give a damn." He grabbed her shoulders. "Do you her me, Jocelyn? I don't give a damn. You've made my life a living hell and I'm tired of it."

"You're serious aren't you?"

He dropped his hands to his sides.

"I'm divorcing you, Jocelyn."

"You will be in for the fight of your life." She said plainly.

"Let me tell you what's going to happen." He felt calmer. "You will get in your beautiful brand new Mercedes that I will let you keep along with the house and a great deal of money that will allow you to live in the comfort you've become accustomed to, sign where my lawyer has indicated, turn the papers into your lawyer and advise him that the divorce will be uncontested."

Now, she was looking at him like he'd lost his mind.

She lifted a brow and gave him a crooked smile. "Is this your first time meeting me?"

"Unfortunately it is not. However, this is your first time meeting me…The new Dixon Phoenix"

She rolled her eyes. "Come on now, really. What are you going to tell our children?"

"We don't have little children anymore. We have grown men who have their own lives." Dixon also wondered what their sons would say, but he was confident that they would be fine. "It's time for me to start living mine, without you."

"That's impossible. You are my husband. There are no divorces in my family."

"I have no problem with you and I being the first. Trust me, Jocelyn; you don't want to fight me on this." She eyed him with such malevolence that it made his skin crawl just knowing he'd shared a life with this woman. Her look also told him that she was bracing for battle.

"Save that look for someone you can intimidate. I want the papers signed by morning."

"Now I know you must have lost your mind."

"Do you know what I know?" He leaned in so close to her that anyone passing by would think he was on the verge of kissing her. "I know you had a child out of wedlock and I also know who the father is and if you don't want everyone else to find out, then I suggest you stop telling me what you think you know about my mind."

Her mouth transformed into a thin line and she stoically opened her car door, got inside and drove away.

Chapter 16

New Orleans

"Are you sure you're ok, Soph?" Alexandra asked from the doorway of the guest room.

"I'm fine, Alex. New Orleans sounds like it will be a great distraction and I'm desperately in need of a distraction."

They were going to drive into New Orleans for dinner and a little fun afterwards.

"Are you sure you don't mind Erika staying here?"

"No, not at all. The more the merrier. We'll make it work. Where is she, anyway?"

"Thanks. She's downstairs doing some stuff for the studio. I just feel better having her here with all of us, after—"

Alex walked in and sat on the bed next to Sophia.

"I'm sorry about Kristina."

"Me too." She responded quietly. Sophia stood, walked to the other side of the bed and opened her suitcase. She needed to change the subject or she would cry again. "What are you wearing?"

"I have a cute skirt I bought in Bermuda a couple of months ago that I've been dying to wear."

"Is it dressy?"

"Not really, I'm wearing sandals with it, but it will be fine for dinner and any place we decide to go afterwards."

"Hmmm…Ok." She wondered if men had this same conversation about what to wear. Sophia pulled a few things out of the suitcase. "It was so hard packing for this trip."

"What do you mean?"

"Well, from New York to Boston was ok, but trying to make sure I had clothes to go from spring weather in the north to spring in the south was another feat altogether. I had to go shopping before I left Boston."

"Yea, the weather is a bit different, but I thought you were flying back to Manhattan before you flew here." Alex picked up one of Sophia's blouses. "This is so cute."

"I got that in a little shop right after we met at the bridal store. Where are Candice and Landon anyway? Is her mom better?"

"Yes, Ms. Lillian is much better. Candice and Landon will meet us in New Orleans."

"Good. I miss them."

"Soooo…what's up with you and Ethan and did he have something to do with why you had packing issues?"

Sophia knew the question was coming, but she was unsure how to answer. She didn't quite know what was going on with Ethan and her.

"What do you mean?"

Alex tilted her head towards Sophia and gave her a wry smile showing one of her golden dimples.

Sophia inhaled deeply, exhaled and flopped herself on the bed. "I don't know." The words were almost a whine.

"It just looks like the two of you arrived here together."

Sophia threw her head back onto a pillow and covered her eyes with her arm.

"We did."

"How'd you manage that, Chica?"

"There's a man stalking me and Ethan wouldn't let me go home after he found out."

"Wait. What?" Alex moved Sophia's arm and tugged on it. "No way, Ma'am. You're going to have to sit up and give me the full unabridged version."

So, Sophia told Alex everything that transpired from that Wednesday night in the club until they left his place Tuesday to travel to Baton Rouge—well, almost everything. She left out the part about their insatiable sex life and Ethan's connection to the Phoenix's.

"It's all your fault." She said, pointing at Alex.

"How's it my fault?"

"If you didn't have such a nice place, I would've grabbed some pizza and headed back to my hotel room instead of going dancing at Cliques."

"Well from what you've said about the poisoning, it was a good thing Ethan was there." Her voice became low and soft. "Do you like him?"

"I don't hate him."

Alex smiled. "That's a start."

Festive music blared from the speakers in the modestly sized establishment. It was the sort of place a person could dress up or down. So she felt comfortable in her yellow sundress and wedged heels. The dress was gathered up one side to the thigh so she wore a pair of cropped leggings underneath.

There was an hour wait for a table for nine at the seafood restaurant they chose in the French Quarter, which was fine because Landon and Candice were still on their way. Sophia wondered who they were bringing with them as she glanced around at all the people happily waiting their turn. She couldn't figure out if it was the bar drinks or if the food was simply worth it. She was coming to the conclusion that it was both. Mountains of food were being placed on tables in front of patrons in the dining room. Her mouth was watering just looking at it. She hadn't had fried seafood in a very long time.

"Ethan, you have to try this." Sophia scooted her bloody Mary over to Ethan so he could take a sip."

"I don't like them."

"Come on, you've got to try it. It's delicious."

He looked hesitant at first, she gave him a playful wink and he placed his lips on the straw, never taking his eyes off of her. She shivered just watching him.

His eyes widened in surprise.

"See, I told ya. It's good huh?"

"Yes, as far as bloody Mary's go."

She took a long sip and closed her lids.

He watched her, feeling slightly jealous of the straw.

"I'll be right back."

Sophia watched Ethan walk through the throng of people and thought he was easily the most handsome guy in the place. Joshua was handsome, sure, but Ethan was the guy who made her pulse quicken. She couldn't' take her eyes off of him. She also saw how many of the women checked him out as he passed. One hussy had the nerve to purposely push herself against him when he tried to get by her.

Sophia raised a brow, though it wasn't jealously that climbed up her back, but rather a sort of elation knowing that he'd confessed he loved *her* and had been dreaming about *her* since that day at the grave yard—not anyone else.

The grave yard.

It was the day she'd finally been able to say goodbye to Sparrow. Her face sobered from the memory, but then quickly shaking her head free of it, she looked around the restaurant again. Her eyes settled on Erika sitting next to her and Sophia's lips lifted into a smile in response to the cheesy grin on Erika's face.

"He's nice." Erika gushed.

"Yes."

"I feel like I'm on vacation instead of out of town for work." She beamed. "Thanks for asking me to come."

Sophia wondered about her young assistant. She hadn't thought about it before, but she really had no idea about Erika's personal life. "I'm glad you could come on such short notice." She hadn't told her about Kristina yet, but knew she would have to soon.

Sophia looked towards the area where the bathrooms were again.

Alex gave Joshua a nudge with her elbow and looked at him.

"How long do you think Ethan and Sophia will pretend nothing is going on?"

Joshua looked at his wife then towards the entrance of the restaurant.

"Oh I say…about five minutes."

She looked up at him then towards the door where he was looking. In walked Candice and Landon with Candice's cousin, Chelsea and a man she didn't know. Joshua stood as the group neared them.

"Who's the guy?" She whispered.

Just then, Landon lifted Alex from the bar stool and squeezed her tight. He sat her on her feet and did the same with Sophia. The two women were the same height.

"Soph! It's so good to see you."

Candice hugged the ladies and they both asked about her mother. She was doing much better and would be able to attend the wedding Saturday.

Sophia introduced Erika to Candice and Landon. They both greeted her with hugs as if she were part of the family.

"We're huggers." Landon exclaimed.

The young woman seemed a bit overwhelmed.

"Nice to meet you both. Congrats on the upcoming wedding."

"Thanks." They said in unison and then kissed each other as if just thinking about the wedding made all their love swell to the surface.

Joshua rolled his eyes at them and then made the introductions for the man who'd come in with Candice and Landon.

"And this ugly fellow is our cousin, Terry Phoenix!" Joshua gave him a good natured slap on the back. The man was a god—just as handsome as the other men in their party. Erika nearly knocked her glass over when she reached to shake his hand. He pretended not to notice.

"Terry, this is my beautiful wife, Alexandra." Joshua announced.

"Beautiful indeed." He said giving her a warm hug.

"And this is my best friend, Sophia." Landon piped in. "The one I was telling you about." Sophia shot Landon a look.

Alex whispered to Joshua, "I don't think it will take a whole five minutes."

Sophia reached for Terry's hand.

"It's nice to meet you, Terry. Don't believe a word he's said about me."

"I have no choice. You are as beautiful as he said." His smile was infectious and she couldn't help the slight color that rose to her cheeks.

Ethan appeared out of nowhere and stood next to her. He thrust out his hand towards Terry.

"Ethan Powers. Landon's friend and business partner. Nice to meet you."

Terry wasn't affronted at all, but Sophia felt as if Ethan had just pissed on her leg to mark his territory. The strange thing about it was she didn't seem to mind.

It was Candice's turn to introduce the woman.

"Everyone this is my cousin Chelsea Carwin-Smith. She flew in from Savannah this morning."

Oh… she's the person who will be staying in the room between Ethan and hers, Sophia thought. She was tall and dark like Candice, but held neither the beauty or sophisticated grace as her cousin. The woman extended a dainty hand out to everyone, but her eyes lingered on Ethan a tad too long. She had a thick southern dialect that seemed exaggerated to Sophia.

"Phoenix…party of nine…Phoenix…party of nine." The hostess called.

"Looks like we got here right on time." Landon stated.

Sophia and Alex grabbed their drinks from the bar and everyone followed the hostess to their table. Just as Sophia was about to whisper something to Ethan, Chelsea linked her arm with Ethan's and pulled him towards the dining area.

"They tell me you used to live in Australia." She bubbled, through her syrup-coated accent.

Ethan glanced at Sophia and saw Terry at her side. Their eyes locked before she turned to Terry who was asking her about her accent.

The table was large and round. Ethan sat next to Sophia and Chelsea sat next to him, while Terry sat on the other side of Sophia.

Chelsea's animated southern drawl was so distracting; Sophia couldn't focus on the menu. The woman seemed to need Ethan's opinion about everything.

"What's good, Alex?" Ethan asked trying to politely ignore Chelsea.

"Everything is great here, but if you can't decide and you love seafood, get the seafood platter." She pointed at a tray going by their table. There's one there.

"So much?" Sophia asked. "Who can eat all of that?"

"You'll be surprised." Alex answered as she swatted away Joshua's pointing finger. "It's sooo good, huh, Candice."

"Yes. It's a local favorite as well as a favorite of tourists." Candice answered her friend.

"I'd never come here until after Alex and I were married and we came back for business with the sports bar." The waiter placed water on the table. Joshua continued, "I hated that I'd missed out on it for so long."

Ethan turned to Sophia who was salivating over a stack of onion rings floating by the table. She mumbled something in Spanish.

"The only time I've heard you speak Spanish is right before you have an orgasm." He whispered.

"Those onion rings might just get me there." She winked.

Oh how he liked her honesty.

"Do you want to split the platter?"

Sophia was sure she'd just heard Chelsea ask Ethan the same thing and wondered what she would say when he split one with her instead.

"Sure." She agreed, closing her menu and placing it on the table.

The waiter arrived. A dark brown *man*, she thought, but wasn't sure. The waiter had perfectly arched eyebrows and flawless makeup, but the voice was definitely male. Only Chelsea seemed shocked by his feminine features and deep voice.

"Well I never." She drawled.

"You should get out more." Sophia said. No one heard her but Ethan and Terry. Terry choked on his water trying to stifle a laugh. Erika was more than happy to pat and rub his back. The others looked at Terry.

"You ok?" Alex asked.

"Yea." He said, after taking a deep cleansing breath.

After Landon told the waiter, Chad was his name, what he wanted to order he looked across the table at Terry.

"Terry, did I tell you our little Sophia here, is a dance instructor to the stars?"

Terry turned to Sophia.

"No you didn't." He replied to Landon but looked at Sophia. "Who was the most interesting person you've danced with?"

"Ethan." The name placed itself on her tongue and walked out of her mouth on its own accord.

The table was silent. Ethan's lips twitched trying to suppress a smile. Terry looked from face to face thinking he'd missed something and was sure he had. Before anyone could respond, Chad was asking Sophia what she wanted for dinner.

Sophia raised a questioning eyebrow towards Ethan for confirmation about the platter.

"We're going to split the seafood platter." Ethan told Chad. He gave Sophia a crooked grin "And an order of onion rings."

"Very good, Sir."

Sophia's cheeks heated. Chad went on to Chelsea and again the rest of the table was silent. Chad gathered the menus and walked away, promising the salads and appetizers would be out shortly.

Joshua, ever the diplomat, spoke first.

"How about we go to our place here in town and just see how interesting our Ethan is on the dance floor."

"Yes, that sounds wonderful." Chelsea looked at Ethan. "I love to dance."

Sophia heard Terry explain to Erika that Joshua and Alex were co-owners of a sports bar not too far from the Quarter. She looked across the table at Landon and saw a familiar frown on his face. He was pissed about something.

Chapter 17

The Challenge

"I'll have to dance for the next five nights to work off that meal." Candice groaned as she rubbed her belly, giving voice to everyone's thoughts.

"I like this place, Alex. It's different from Cliques, but just as nice." Sophia added.

And it was. Cliques was subtle and chic whereas Lagniappe's atmosphere was a bit more rowdy, but in a good way. Everyone was friendly. The music was lively and the décor was classic New Orleans.

"Thanks, Soph. My partner and I worked hard to create a welcoming atmosphere."

"Where're the guys?" Chelsea asked, looking around the place.

"I think they thought it would be easier to get the drinks from the bar than to wait for a waitress." Candice said to her cousin. "It's pretty crowded tonight."

"Geez Alex, ya'll must be rolling in dough if your place is this crowded during the week. How much money does this place clear in a week?"

Even Erika, who was the youngest in the bunch, thought Chelsea's comment was rude and tacky. Sophia gave Chelsea a hard disapproving stare and Candice shook her head as she let out an annoying sigh.

"We're lucky enough to have tourist all year long." Alex commented dryly and looked at her nails. "I can't wait until our mani and pedi day." She said, ignoring her question. Sophia's smile and nod confirmed her agreement.

Alex remembered Candice's cousin, Chelsea and had never really cared for her. She was always too loud, too talkative and too forward—just way too much.

Candice looked at her friend and gave her a look that said, "Sorry."

Everyone except Chelsea became occupied with rocking and bouncing to the beat to fill the awkward moment. Alex received a text and wondered who would be texting her so late in the evening.

It was from Candice. The text read:

**My mom made me invite her...URGH!
She's been getting on my
nerves since she got here
this morning.**

Seductive Pleasures

Alex looked at her friend and rolled her eyes to the ceiling. She slipped her phone back into her purse and watched the dancers on the floor. Sophia saw the subtle eye-play between the women and figured they were "telepathically" talking about Chelsea. She also wondered what was taking the men so long. The anticipation of being in Ethan's arms again was making her feel tingly and nervous.

It seemed like forever since they'd touched, but in actuality it had only been a few hours. But still, she wanted to feel him hold her on the dance floor, not sure how he would react with an audience.

"What the hell is going on between you and Sophia? Just a few days ago, I would've given my left nut to wager you'd never even had a decent conversation." Landon's gray eyes were intense with concern. "Now you're the most interesting person she's ever danced with?"

Both men stood about the same height and had similar builds. Landon's hair was cut close to his head and Ethan's was a mass of curls, not unlike Joshua's, but longer.

Ethan was standing face to face with his brother.

His brother.

He had a brother—two in fact. It was the first time the thought didn't leave a bad taste in his mouth. His mom was gone, but he still had family. Even Terry, a stranger to him before tonight, was his cousin.

"It's complicated."

"No shit!"

Ethan wondered if he should tell Landon and Joshua the entire story before the wedding or wait. He would hate to wait and Landon hate him for standing up for him knowing the truth. Everything was starting to feel like a lie.

Landon's cell rang. It was his mother.

"What the hell does she want?"

There was a patio on his left so he stepped outside to take the call although the music was almost just as loud.

"What?" Joshua asked, concerned by the look on Landon's face when he returned.

"That was Mom."

"What did she want at this hour?"

"She said Dad is having a mid-life crisis and has asked her for a divorce."

"What?...Why?...What did you say?" Joshua's surprise made him trip over his questions. He knew Landon had mixed feelings about their dad and mom's marriage.

"I said, 'I love you mom, but it's about damn time.'"

"What's going on here? We thought you guys were getting drinks."

Awkward silence hung even in the mist of the music and noise of the crowd.

The men looked around at each other before Joshua finally spoke up.

"Apparently the bartenders are slammed." He said to his wife with a wink and a playful nudge with his hip.

Alex frowned. There was something he wasn't telling her. She knew her husband too well. She also knew him well enough to know that if it was something important, he would tell her later, so she let it go.

"Is that right?" She leaned up on tip toes and gave him a kiss before she walked behind the bar and yelled across to them. "What's your pleasure?" She only had eyes for Joshua.

Alexandra worked as a bartender during her years of law school and had become quite good at it. They saw her wave at one of the bartenders closest to her and the show was on. Not only did they get their drinks but they got them in grand style. The crowd

227

around the bar cheered and begged for more as they usually did. Alex made a few more drinks by tossing bottles and throwing ice from one bartender to another and then called it quits so they all could hit the dance floor.

"Did you know she could do that?" Ethan asked Sophia when they walked to the floor.

"No idea."

"Do you have any hidden talents?" He asked right before he held her close and began moving to the sultry jazz tune.

She pulled back slightly. "Tons." They both laughed as he twirled her around.

"And you?" She pressed her body against his and kissed the area of his neck just below his ear, then whispered, "Do you have any hidden talents."

How could a woman make him feel so fearless and yet so powerless? He relished the comfort of her nearness. Ethan folded her into his arms and rocked slowly, ignoring the upbeat tempo of the song the band was now playing. Over the past few days he'd exhausted many of his hidden talents. Some he was not even aware he possessed until she was tangled in his limbs.

"With you, they don't stay hidden for long." He finally said.

Seductive Pleasures

She looked up at him, grabbed her bottom lip with her teeth and slowly released it. That simple act was Ethan's undoing. Desire pulled his mouth to hers until he was able to grab her glossed lip in a gentle bite before they melted into a kiss right there on the dance floor.

Oh how Ethan wanted this woman. He was sure he would never have a dull day again. She fit perfectly in his arms. This little slip of a woman was quickly becoming a huge part of his life. He loved her. He wanted to take care of her and most importantly, he wanted her to be his family and keep her safe. He loved Sophia Ilarraza. Now if she would only love him back.

"I love that you can dance."

"That's a start." He whispered.

She reached up and fingered the hair at the back of his head and he held her tighter. Never did he want to let her go. So he told her.

"I don't ever want to let you go."

He thought he heard her say, "Don't," but it could have just been wishful thinking.

"You once told me that you could sing and play the piano." She whispered near his ear.

He grinned. "I did, but that was an incentive for you to dance for me."

She tossed her head over her shoulder. "There is a piano and a microphone right there." Her eyes twinkled with the challenge.

Ethan slid his arms from her back and down her sides, gave her the sweetest kiss she'd ever tasted and stepped away from her.

Stunned, she watched him walk towards the band and whisper something to the piano player. The throng of people surrounding her, faded from view when she saw him slide into position at the piano. His eyes found hers and held them with an air of expectancy.

It was not until she heard the piano riff that she was able to look away. His voice rose above the crowd. Slow, raspy and strong. It moved her. Her eyes moved to him again.

He wanted her to dance for him.

So she did.

Her fingers reaching to the sky, her body moved like a palm blowing in the ocean's breeze. He sang a song she loved, "Beneath Your Beautiful," by the British singer, Labrinth.

She didn't see the crowd part to watch her. She didn't see Alex and the rest of the group stand speechless at the sight of them both. She didn't see the woman take the stage to sing the female part of the duet.

All she saw was Ethan.

He wanted her to dance for him and his words stirred her. The keys of the piano vibrated along her spine and bent her to their will. Reaching to her ankle she lifted her leg until her foot stopped just above her head causing a perfect standing split. She didn't hear the awe from the crowd. She only heard him—his voice seducing her into a rhythmic banter only he could understand. Many of the men watching were thrilled to be able to witness the conversation.

Thanking God for Mrs. Viola and her relentless piano instruction, he was glad his fingers could dance across the keys pretty much on their own.

What made him think he would be able to just watch Sophia dance and not be moved to the point of wanting to make love to her until sunrise?

She was moving art.

She inspired him.

So much so that he found himself singing in public, something he never did. To him, he was not singing for anyone but her. He'd seen her dance before but tonight she didn't dance, she spoke to him with her body. He realized it was the only way she knew how to let go; the only way she could reveal what she always seem to keep just beneath the surface.

He listened and wanted to weep.

When the singing was done, he went to her, held her against his heart and felt the cadence of the mingled beats. They had a rhythm that was unique. It was undeniable.

The crowd erupted but neither of them noticed.

He loved this woman. There was so much he wanted to say, so he talked to her in the language she knew best. He danced with her.

It was a fun upbeat dance that had them spinning, dizzy and laughing by the end of it.

They were walking back to join the rest of the group when Sophia saw Chelsea fade into the crowd. She leaned into Ethan and said, "She's got her eyes on you."

Ethan rolled his eyes knowing exactly who Sophia was talking about.

"You better be careful tonight; her room is right next door."

"And if she came to my room…what would you say?"

"Get out; we're busy."

"That's my girl."

For some reason when he called her his girl it felt like humming bird wings flapping in the sun over a beautiful flower.

"You and Ethan look great out there, Sophia." Candice yelled over the music.

"Thanks." She thought they looked great out there too.

Sophia looked around wondering where Chelsea was and noticed the mural on the wall behind the bar area that extending along the length of part of the dance floor. She turned to Alex.

"Wow, Alex! The artwork almost comes alive."

Sophia walked over to a portion of the wall and was mesmerized, almost haunted by the images. They weren't the usual French Quarter scenes, but rather paintings of open windows with views of late great jazz musicians as if they were creating new music to play.

How in the hell could an artist capture the essence of that?

Sophia rubbed her hand along a young Dizzy Gillespie holding his horn in one hand and a pencil in the other, while reaching to write down notes. He was sitting at a beat up wooden kitchen table with no matching chairs and wore a wrinkled white shirt, black slacks and brown house slippers.

"This is remarkable." She commented with great admiration of such artistry.

"Yes, it is." Alex responded, looking at Candice. "My best friend is quite the artist."

Sophia spun around to face the ladies again.

"You did this, Candice?"

"Guilty."

"Oh my God," she breathed as if she was trying not to disturb Dizzy at work. "This is wonderful."

Just then, the waitress stopped with a tray of drinks for them. Each lady took her glass and looked at each other.

"What shall we drink to?" Asked Sophia.

Alex raised her glass and the others did the same. "Let's drink to good food, good friends, good music and being able to enjoy it with some very handsome men." At that moment the guys were walking back into the club area from the other side of the establishment where they were probably watching Sports Center on ESPN. The ladies looked at them, looked at each other, clinked their glasses and cheered, "Here, here!"

"Where's Terry?" Candice asked.

"He's off somewhere with Erika." Landon responded as he scanned the crowd. "Where's Chelsea?"

"She's off sulking somewhere because Sophia won't let her dance with Ethan." Alex blurted in jest, but they all laughed a little too hard for it not to be true.

Sophia simply tipped her glass towards her, smiled and took a drink.

"Did you have a good time, Phia?"

"I did."

They sat on the porch swing where he'd held her earlier that day, but now they rocked in the cool of the night. It was that time when it was too late to be night and too early to be morning. The house was quiet and Ethan figured they were probably the only ones awake.

"Are you worried about your friend?"

"Yes, a little. But Kristina is a fighter. I believe she will bounce back from this."

"Have you told Erika?"

"Not yet. There just never was a good time to tell her today…If that's such a thing." She snuggled a little closer to him, not wanting to talk about anything heavy. "What's your favorite smell?"

235

Ethan chuckled softly.

"Hmmm…I'm not sure. No one has ever asked me that before."

"Think about it." She said. "Do you have a favorite smell from your childhood?"

"Yes."

"What is it?" She turned to look at his face and even in the shadows he was the most handsome man ever created.

"The smell of gardenias." He said it so softly she studied him a moment.

"Why? What does the smell remind you of?"

"Happiness."

She laughed quietly. "You're not the cookie cutter guy, Mr. Powers... Why happiness?"

"They were my mother's favorites." Even as his eyes looked off into the distance his lips lifted slightly at the corners and his face brightened. "They give me a terrible headache…but they made her happy."

Sophia's smile reflected his.

"What about you? What's your favorite smell?"

Without hesitation she declared, "A fresh box of crayons."

"Crayons?"

"Yep."

"Ok." Silence settled between them for a moment. "I like you, little lady."

She leaned close to his ear and whispered. "Make love to me, Ethan."

Ethan stood and took her hand. He looked at the woman he loved and his fingers, his mouth, his tongue ached to brand every part of her as his. Any place she looked or touched on her body, he wanted her to remember he'd been there, claiming every last inch.

His head dipped to taste her and she welcomed the kiss, latching on to his tongue greedily. He pulled back shaking his head.

"No."

"No?" Confusion clouded her features. "Don't you want me?"

"My way." His words were not meant to be challenged.

She opened her mouth to protest, but he placed a finger on her lips to still whatever she'd planned to say.

"I said, *my way*."

She was lost in the depths of his dark eyes.

He leaned in to kiss her again. She let him guide it and knew she would drown in the sweetness of it. He sampled her lips, her tongue...everything he tasted, so painstakingly slow that her body hummed and waves of pleasure climbed so high that she just knew she would break apart when they came crashing down.

This was the same man who'd held and stroked her so fiercely that he left bruises. Now the tenderness in which he kissed and touched her was so erotic that she knew when they came together this time, it would be different. It would be an unspoken confirmation of his feelings for her. And even though she hadn't really admitted it to herself, there was no way she wouldn't be able to physically confirm her feelings for him as well.

After he'd gotten his taste of her and gave her a hint of what was to come, he led her into the house and up the stairs to his room. To both of their surprise, Chelsea was tapping on Ethan's door wearing a night gown that barely covered parts that should be covered.

Sophia raised a brow and dragged her eyes from the woman's pouty lips to her bare feet.

So typical...

A feeling claimed her that she'd never felt before. It wasn't jealousy because the woman wasn't worth the kind of energy jealously exhausts. What she felt was possessiveness.

She felt the sudden urge to *piss on his leg*.

"Is there something *we* can do for you, Chelsea?" Sophia felt Ethan's arm claimed her waist and it felt good. It felt…right.

Chelsea's eyes darted from Sophia to Ethan and she had the good sense to look embarrassed.

"Sorry, I didn't know."

"Sure you did, but you thought you'd give it a shot anyway." Sophia looked at the woman, daring her to deny it. Chelsea looked away.

Sophia smiled sweetly, looked up and held Ethan's eyes for a moment. She gently slid the back of her hand down the side of his face. "I don't blame you; he's gorgeous."

She turned back to Chelsea. "Isn't he?" The woman scowled at Sophia.

"You don't have to say it… I know." Chelsea began to back away, but Sophia's next words stayed her. "And just so we're absolutely clear…since *you didn't know*." She said in a mocking tone. "Other than being gorgeous, he's also mine." She felt his fingers squeeze her slightly.

"And because you're Candice's cousin and I'm a lady, I won't out right call you a bitch, because…well…frankly, I don't know you like that, but this scene right here," Sophia swirled a finger, "this has trifling-bitch tendencies written all over it."

Silence.

"So I suggest, that next time you need something in the middle of the night... you don't come knocking here...not on *this* door."

Chapter 18

The Phoenix Brothers

"How did you know?"

"It was coincidence, really." Ethan didn't want any lies between Landon and himself, but didn't really know how to tell him how he'd outsmarted Franklin, without giving away *all* the details.

"How so?"

At the club last night, Landon told Ethan he wanted to meet with him in the morning to go over details of the contracts with Bruce Franklin and anything else Landon missed while away. Ethan hated leaving Sophia in bed, especially since her legs were tangled with his and he remembered clearly how they'd gotten that way. Plus he hadn't had much sleep, but he knew he needed to update Landon more thoroughly on business.

He still had a hard time believing what she'd said to Chelsea. His head swelled with whatever kind of stuffing the ego is made of, when she put Chelsea in her place and claimed him as hers.

Somehow he would have to convince Sophia he was truly sincere about loving her. She never wanted to talk about anything in her past or about the future.

She was content, it seemed, with just living in the present, which was fine but he needed to know if he was wasting his time.

Just as he thought about the possibility of not pursuing Sophia, he knew there was no way he could possibly let her go. They fit together, whether she knew it or not, although he was sure she knew it too, but was afraid of something. He wished he knew what.

"Some associates of mine had dealings with old man Franklin and got screwed over, nearly losing everything." Ethan sat on the corner of the desk while Landon slowly browsed the books on the shelves.

Joshua walked into the room Ethan was sure Alex's father had once used as an office and greeted them both. Law books lined one wall and accolades from a prestigious law career on another. There was a window overlooking at least a couple acres of lush green grass spotted with trees— magnolias, according to Alex. The office and view was magnificent like the rest of the house.

"Am I interrupting anything?" Joshua asked the men after seeing the crease in Landon's forehead.

"Well it looks like my partner has saved our company from ruin." Landon bolstered as he walked over and patted Ethan on the back."

"Ruin?" Joshua asked sitting in one of the two chairs in front of the large desk.

Landon scratched his head and took the seat next to his brother. "Yea, apparently Franklin was trying to bamboozle us by creating a situation for Enrich Corp. to buy him out then having the company revert back to him after two years."

Joshua looked confused.

"How wouldn't you have known ahead of time?"

"Loop holes, embedded so deep into the fine print, it would be nearly impossible to catch if you weren't looking for it." Landon explained to Joshua what Ethan had explained to him.

"How did you catch it, Ethan?" Joshua asked.

Just then, Alex opened the door of the office and all three men looked up and smiled when they saw her.

Alex looked from one man to the other. Her return smile of greeting turned into one of surprise.

"My goodness," she said with her hand on her chest. "You all have the exact same smile." She took a few steps into the office. "I don't know why I've never noticed before…Come to think about it, Ethan you look as if you could be related to them." They looked at each other. She walked to the shelves of books, pulled a couple and put one back. "I guess you've been spending too much time together." She said over her shoulder. "Here it is." Mumbling to herself before looking at the men again. "I'm sorry if I interrupted you, but I've been looking for something and I think the answer is in here." She waved a hand. "Carry on."

Ethan had forgotten Alex still practiced law on occasion. She walked out and he looked at the two men viewing him expectantly.

It was time to tell them.

"I have something a little difficult to tell the two of you," He stood and walked over to the standing globe in the room and gave it a spin, not sure how to initiate the topic that had been foremost in his mind since he could remember. "and I'm not sure where to start."

"About the business deal?" Landon asked, then met his brother's confused expression that mirrored his own. They both looked at Ethan and waited.

Ethan faced the men again. "No...well yes... in a way, but there's so much more to it."

"Ok." It was Joshua who spoke.

Ethan began. "I don't know if you knew, but I was adopted."

There was a pause while Ethan looked from one man to the other.

"Yes, I knew." Landon confessed.

This bit of news surprised Ethan.

"You did?"

"Yes, I had you checked out." He said plainly.

Ethan raised a brow. He'd had no idea Landon had him investigated before they went into business together and wasn't quite sure how he felt about it at first, then realized he probably would've done the same thing.

"Yes, of course. I didn't know much about you. I wasn't going to invest my life savings into a new business with someone who I couldn't trust.

Ethan sat on the edge of the desk again, wondering how much Landon knew about him.

"So, I take it that you found out I was trustworthy." The words came out more harshly than he intended.

"I found out that your business dealings in Brisbane, Australia and those in England were squeaky clean."

Ethan held no anxiety about that. He prided himself on his business ethics, which made him wonder if he truly would've been able to go through with his plans of sabotaging Enrich Corp. He'd said it was because of Sophia and the kindness of all the Phoenix men, but could he have actually done it?

Joshua's next words stunned Ethan.

"Ethan, do you know who your birth mother is?"

Ethan wasn't sure, but something in Joshua's face suggested that *he* knew.

"Yes I do." He stated, cautiously.

Joshua and Landon shared a look.

Ethan eased off the desk. "You know, don't you?"

"Yes." Both men responded.

Ethan didn't know whether to be relieved or upset. His eyes darted from one man to the other. Landon's lips were set in a tiny smirk and Joshua's features were unreadable.

They knew he was their brother.

They knew.

"Why didn't you…wait…" Ethan's thick brows bunched together. "Was the Franklin deal some sort of test of my loyalty?"

"Not exactly." Landon answered. Still seated, he linked his fingers in front of him. "I never questioned your loyalty." He looked at Joshua and moved his finger from one to the other. "Rather, *we* never questioned your loyalty." Turning back to Ethan he said, "I knew there was something fishy with Franklin, but couldn't put my finger on it. I went over all the documents thoroughly, but came up with nothing."

"And your lawyers?" Ethan asked. Because the men dealt with two different aspects of the company, they each used their own team of lawyers.

"They couldn't come up with anything that corroborated with my gut."

"But you were going to go through with it anyway."

"No. Like I said, I had you checked out and from the information I found out about you, your specialty is finding the thread that fell off the needle in the haystack."

Ethan smiled, but he was still unsure as to why Landon left the deal in his hands.

Landon continued, "When Candice's mom got sick, I figured instead of killing the deal, I would just put it in your hands to see if you could find the thread and see if we could beat Bruce Franklin in his own dirty game." Landon made a gesture with his hands. "And you did."

"Why didn't you just ask me to help you with it?"

"Your plate was just as full as mine for a while."

It had never occurred to Ethan that the men knew he was their brother. He didn't know what to say or what to do.

How much did they know?

"Ethan," Joshua spoke as if seeing the question in his eyes. "I only found out a few weeks ago."

Landon spoke again. "So to answer your question, no, I wasn't testing your loyalty to the company or to the family; I was testing your skills in dissecting a contract."

"You should've been."

Landon looked confused.

"Should've been what?"

"Testing my loyalty." Ethan wanted them to know it all.

Both men sat up straighter in their chairs.

"What do you mean?" Landon asked.

So he told them. He told them how he'd planned for revenge on a family that he thought had wronged him.

"So what changed your mind?" Joshua asked.

"All of you. The two of you treated me like family… Dixon has been more than kind… and Sophia." He nearly whispered her name. "I tried not to want her, but it was impossible.

"So you have feelings for her or is it merely a physical attraction?" Landon wanted to know the extent of their relationship.

"I'm in love with her."

Joshua nodded his head. "And she loves you." He said flatly.

Ethan's eyes told Joshua that he didn't believe him. So Joshua told him what the two of them couldn't figure out on their own. "I can see it all over her face. The other day when she received news about her friend…she wanted only you to comfort her."

"What? Wait…What are you talking about?" Landon asked confused.

So Ethan told them both about the guy stalking Sophia, the poisoning and her stay in the hospital.

"Man, why didn't you tell me about this? Sophia is my best friend."

"At first I didn't think there was anything to tell, and when there was, she didn't want me to say anything. Though, Dixon knows."

"How the hell does Dad know?" Landon asked the question, but Ethan could see the same question in Joshua's eyes.

"He happened to be at the hospital when I was speaking with the doctor about Sophia. And Sophia knew you were busy with wedding plans and Candice's mom…"

Ethan's words halted. He watched Joshua stand, walk around the chairs and stop in front of him. His expression was passive so he didn't know how to respond to him standing there.

"Thank you, Ethan." He said, finally as he extended a hand to him.

"For what?" Ethan took his firm grip in his and shook it.

"For finally shedding some light on what's been wrong with Landon all these years."

"And what's that?" Both Ethan and Landon asked simultaneously.

"He has been suffering for the classic middle child syndrome."

They all laughed and Joshua gave Ethan a huge bear hug and said, "Welcome to the family, Brother."

And just like that, all his worries about what they would think or do, evaporated.

Landon stood and gave him the same welcome. Never would he have thought that he would find brothers so willing to accept him into their family. Literally with open arms.

Ethan's throat felt tight and raw from his brother's reactions.

A thought occurred to Ethan. Landon mentioned he'd found out about his birth mother, but he wondered if they knew the identity of his birth father.

Joshua stepped away while the other two men talked about Bruce Franklin's response to the new contracts Ethan sent to Franklin's office. He turned suddenly.

"Does dad know?" He walked towards them. "About Mom…and…you?" He said, pointing at Ethan.

"Yes, I told him Saturday morning."

"Is that why he filed for divorce?" It was Landon who asked the question they all wondered. "Come to think about it, Mom squawked about Dad starting a rumor about her so she would sign the papers."

"Do you know anything about that, Ethan?" Joshua asked him.

Ethan had a pretty good idea about the leverage Dixon was using to get her to give him a quiet divorce.

"I'm sure it has something to do with my father."

"Your father?" Both asked.

"Yes, my father, Cortland Phoenix."

Chapter 19

Uncle Cortland

Stunned silence lay over the room.

Apparently Landon's investigators did not glean that bit of information about him; Ethan thought. From their previous conversations, especially when they went out sailing, the Phoenix brothers had nothing but nice things to say about their Uncle Cortland. He'd practically raised them due to their own father's absence in their lives.

While their father worked, Cortland taught them how to sail, showed up at little league games and gave them advice about girls. He was also the reason both men were able to enjoy so much freedom in their career choices. Cortland had left all his money to his nephews.

Ethan had listened to the stories and instead of feeling cheated and spiteful, he was further convinced that Cortland didn't know of his existence.

Cortland Phoenix was a man who made it his life's mission to care for others, even strangers. So, Ethan was sure that if he'd known he had a son, he would have been there for him. The more he knew about Cortland, the more he hated Jocelyn for giving him up and denying him such a man in his life.

If it weren't for the letters he'd found, he would not have understood how Cortland and Jocelyn could have made a baby.

The office door opened and three heads poked in.

"Enough business for now, we have a bunch of wedding stuff to—" Candice's words were silenced by the looks on the men's faces.

"What?" Alex stepped inside the office. "What's wrong?"

The men looked at each other for a brief moment before Landon stretched out his arm and beckoned his fiancé to his side.

"C'mon in, Baby. This concerns you too." He looked at the other women. "All of you. Where's everyone else?"

"I think Chelsea is still getting her beauty sleep and Terry and Erika are in the kitchen eating breakfast." Candice told her future husband.

Since Sophia was included in the conversation she knew they must've been discussing Ethan and his parentage. She walked over and stood next to him. Her hand touched his forearm gently while her eyes held a question. She wanted to know if it was ok that she was included. He smiled and placed his hand on hers.

She let out a breath she didn't realize she was holding. He squeezed her hand and she looked at him and nodded.

The others watched the subtle interplay between the couple. Candice and Alex waited expectantly as Landon began to speak.

"I've known a while but Joshua only found out a few weeks ago that Ethan, here, is our big brother." Both women only lifted their brows in response. Landon looked at Sophia. "And I take it from the lack of surprise on your face, Soph, that you already know?"

She looked up at Ethan; he gave her a hint of a nod. She turned to Landon. "Yes. Ethan has told me the whole story." Landon nodded.

Sophia continued, "And since you are not surprised by that, I take it that you know what's going on with me?"

"Yes." He responded. "Ethan told Josh and me a little while ago…Are you ok?"

"I'm fine."

Alex gave her a reassuring smile.

Candice saw the looks between Sophia and Alex. "Whoa…What?" Candice added, folding her arms across her chest. "It seems that everyone knows bits and pieces except me. I would like to be enlightened on what's going on with Sophia."

So for the next few minutes they caught the women up on what was going on, including the phone call from Jocelyn the night before. That bit of news was a surprise to Sophia as well.

"A divorce?" Alex asked Joshua.

"Yes."

"How do you feel about your parents getting a divorce?"

"Pretty much how Landon feels." He tilted his chin towards his brother.

"It's about damn time." Landon stated.

"Landon!" Candice scolded him.

"Candice, you and everyone else knows that Mom is a monster."

"She's not a *monster*." She tried to find a softer word. "Maybe a little overbearing."

"Whatever kind of sweet little spin you want to put on it, you go right on ahead. But you know her. You've witnessed with your own eyes and ears how hateful she can be." All Candice could do was nod her head in agreement. "We've not gotten along over the years, but Dad deserves better. I believe he deserves a real shot at happiness."

Joshua nodded.

Ethan couldn't believe people could feel such disdain towards their mother. He had to admit that he thought Jocelyn Phoenix was cruel and nasty as well, but he had valid reasons; she'd given him away and never tried to search for him. But he figured his brothers had their own reasons as well. He hadn't grown up with her as they had and experienced the full brunt of her behavior.

"If you ask me, I think he's in love with his secretary, Gloria." All eyes turned to Sophia.

"What makes you say that, Sophia?" Joshua asked her with a short laugh as if the prospect was a little ridiculous.

"I saw the two of them at the benefit last year…I'm not saying I think they're fooling around, but there's definitely something there."

Silence rose for a few moments as they all seemed to let Sophia's comments settle in their heads.

All the ladies had taken a seat by then. Alex in her dad's chair behind the desk and Sophia and Candice in the seats previously occupied by Landon and Joshua. The men naturally migrated and stood next to them.

Landon broke the silence.

"Now, ladies you are all up to speed. My brother," All smiles were directed at Ethan. "was just filling us in on the rest when you graced us with your beauty."

"Is that a nice way of saying, 'when you interrupted us?'" Candice asked as she leaned back and looked up at Landon standing behind her.

He touched his chest in a "who me" gesture.

Sophia reached up and squeezed the hand Ethan had resting on the back of her chair. He gave her a faint smile.

All eyes were on Ethan and it made him feel uncomfortable talking about something that had been so private to him for so long. He took a deep breath and began.

"It wasn't easy finding out who my birth mother was. You would be surprised at how many babies are dropped off at convents." The women shook their heads solemnly. "It turned out that my case was a bit different. Instead of being dropped off on the door step, so to speak, someone paid one of the nuns to take me."

He paused. "It was apparently a large sum. Large enough for one of the nuns to remember the incident." Ethan stared down at Sophia's neck and concentrated on keeping his fingers from tracing the line of it. "The nun revealed the name of a doctor and it took some digging after that, but the doctor was friends with some relatives of Jocelyn's. The birth was never recorded, but the doctor confessed to everything…for a fee of course."

"So you don't have a birth certificate?" Alex asked the question.

"Yes, I do. My adoptive mother's name is on my latest one, however, before that, my birth certificate was created after the convent received me. The mother and father are listed as John Doe and Jane Doe. The birthday is when they found me."

"How interesting. I've never thought about birth certificates for abandoned children, before." A sharp frown appeared on her face. "I'm sorry, Ethan. I guess that was a bit insensitive of me."

"No, not at all, Alex. It's natural curiosity." He gave her a reassuring smile.

"There it is again." She said.

"What?" Ethan asked.

"That smile. You all have the exact same smile." She looked at each man and as if on cue, they smiled in response. "See."

Sophia and Candice looked around and agreed.

"I found out during the investigation when my actual birthday is, though I still celebrate the day my mom adopted me as my official birthday."

"When is it?" Landon asked.

"July 5th."

"Do you mind if we celebrate it this year?"

Ethan was so overwhelmed by the question that he wasn't sure if he could respond. Sophia squeezed his hand again.

"No." His voice cracked. He cleared his throat. "No, I don't mind."

"How did you find out who your father was?" Joshua asked, breaking the tension.

"When Mr. and Mrs. Crocker died, their belongings were auctioned off, because no relatives claimed the estate."

Joshua and Landon looked at one another, confused.

"Who?" Landon asked.

"They were the relatives Jocelyn lived with when she was pregnant, David and Lucy Crocker."

"I've never heard those names in my life." He looked at his brother. "Have you, Josh?"

"No."

Ethan looked from one man to the other and continued.

"The housekeeper kept some old trunks. In the trunks were letters between Jocelyn and Cortland."

"Cortland?" Alex looked at her husband. "Your Uncle Cortland…Dixon's brother?"

"Yes." Ethan answered for him.

"Apparently Cortland and Jocelyn knew each other before your dad and she got together." Ethan saw Joshua frown but kept on with his story. "Courtland thought she was in Europe touring for a year. She was in love with him but he didn't feel the same. Apparently they'd gotten together only the one time and he'd put an end to it right after."

"She never told him?" Candice asked.

"No. She never told anyone. I don't even think her parents knew."

"How did she end up with Dad?" Joshua asked.

"According to the letters, she married him to spite Cortland. I guess she figured if she married his brother that would pay him back for not wanting her."

"Damn."

Ethan couldn't tell which of his brothers uttered the single word.

"Apparently they were a good match for both families. When I talked to your dad, he said he went along with it because she was beautiful and he wanted to please his parents."

260

"Wow. I guess arranged marriages were still pretty common... Especially in their social class." Alex commented.

"He said he hadn't known that Cortland even knew Jocelyn before they were engaged." Ethan took a deep breath. "Well, that's the whole story. I hadn't planned on revealing it before the wedding. I didn't want anything to take away for your day." He said looking at Candice and Landon.

"Thank you for sharing your story with us, Ethan. I am proud to call you my brother and have you stand up for me on our wedding day."

And with that, he was officially welcomed into the family with lots of hugs and kisses. He was overwhelmed, but was also acutely aware that Sophia never left his side.

Chapter 20

Pocket-Sized Honeys

Candice needed to check on the last minute arrangements for the wedding and they also needed to pick up the dresses that had been shipped to a bridal boutique in town. The first stop was the florist. Erika stayed at the house. Going over the contracts was very tedious. She was calculating the fees and organizing Sophia's calendar with the dates the studio needed her. Alex promised to review the contracts before Sophia returned them to the studio executives. More like insisted rather than volunteering.

The florist was an older woman with the kindest brown eyes, Sophia had ever seen. She seemed to know everything there was to know about flowers. While she showed Candice some of the arrangements, Alex and Sophia wandered through the shop.

Alex brushed her fingertips along the unopened buds of a bunch of pink roses. "Ahhhchooo!"

"Bless you." Sophia offered.

"There's no way I could work in here."

"Are you allergic to flowers?"

"Not a moderate amount, but this," she said with a wave, "is more than a moderate amount."

Sophia pulled a travel-sized pack of tissue out of her large leather bag that matched her orange sandals.

"Thanks." Alex said with the tissue up to her nose and moving away from the roses. She tucked it into her pocket and raised serious eyes to Sophia. "How is your friend Kristina?"

"Much better. I talked to her mom and she says they've moved her to a regular room.

"That's good."

"It'll take a while, of course, for her to heal."

Sophia stared at nothing at all and frowned. Alex placed a hand on her friend's forearm. "It's not your fault, Soph."

Sophia inhaled slowly and placed her hand over Alex's. "I know, but—"

"But nothing. It is not your fault!" They both looked around hoping no one was listening to their conversation. In a softer tone, Alex asked, "Have the police found the creep who did that to her?"

"Ethan called Det. Davis this morning and he said there were no leads and nothing connecting Kristina's attack with the man who's stalking me."

Neither of the women said anything. They walked towards the back of the store and saw Candice and Chelsea still speaking with the florist.

Alex, grabbed Sophia by the elbow and pulled her out of view of the women talking in the back.

"Sooo…What's going on with you and Chelsea?" Alex whispered.

"What do you mean?" Sophia suppressed the smile she held inside.

"She's treating you like you made her your bitch."

Sophia burst out laughing.

"What did you do?" Her friend asked again, pointedly.

Sophia really liked Alex. She hadn't had a good friend since she was in high school. Sure, she hung out with Kristina sometimes, but she wasn't someone that she truly considered as one of her friends. In fact, she didn't have any, though lately she found herself confiding in Alex more and more. She knew could trust her.

"Who me?"

"Yes, you. I can see the devilment in your eyes."

"Devilment? How old are you?"

Alex laughed. "Lots of people tell me I have an old soul. I guess because I spent so much time with my dad and his friends when I was growing up."

Seductive Pleasures

Sophia picked up a carnation and inhaled the sweet and tangy aroma. She placed it back in the container.

"Don't ignore me." Alex shot at her with a nudge.

Sophia rolled her eyes just as a young man walked into the flower shop and eyed the two of them like they were on display. They both placed their hands on their hips and met his gaze.

"Oooh wee! Pocket-sized honeys."

Sophia and Alex turned and exchanged a look then looked at the teenager with his pants hanging off of his behind. He couldn't be more than sixteen.

"You got a man, Lil Mamma?" He was directing his comment to Alex.

She cocked her head to the side and stared at him with a look of disbelief that he had the nerve to even try to talk to her. She had shoes older than him.

"Yes, I'm married."

He looked her up and down slowly.

"Your husband is a lucky man." His eyes then fell on Sophia. "How you doing, Sweet Thang?"

"I'm fine, and you?" She said, trying to suppress her laughter.

"Aww Lawd, y'all killin' me! You got an accent. I don't even want to know if you got a man, because if I had you, I'd have to fight brothers e'eryday to keep'em off of *you*!"

They watched the boy look them up and down again then walk over to the counter and yell for his grandma. This was apparently her shop.

They both laughed at being hit on by a kid.

"So?" Alex asked Sophia.

"What?"

"You're going to tell me what happened or do I need to get Bruh Man over there to sweet talk you into it?"

"Dios, Alex. You're not going to let it go are you?"

"I'm a lawyer, ma'am. Please do not forget that I'm trained to know when someone is lying."

"Noted."

"Now spill it, Chica!

Sophia gave her an exasperated sigh. "She's avoiding me because I told her off when she came to Ethan's door half naked last night."

Alex slammed her hand to her mouth.

"She didn't?" She exclaimed incredulously— her hand still slapped over her mouth.

"She did."

"Oh my God. What did you tell her?"

"I told her that yes, I know he is beautiful, but she better not bring herself to his door again, because he's mine." Sophia picked up another flower. "Plus I kinda called her a trifling bitch."

"To be a fly on the wall." Alex's dimples gave evidence that she found the situation quite humorous. "What did she do?"

"She took her fake ass Southern accent to her room."

"And is he?"

"Is he what?" Her eyebrows crinkled in confusion.

"Yours?"

"I just told her that to piss her off." She put the flower back and then turned to Alex. "I'm sorry Alex, but I can't stand that heifer."

All humor left her face. "Me either and Candice knows it. She can't stand her either, but her mom always invites her to stuff and like a lonely puppy she always shows up. Mrs. Carwin thinks we're good influences for her, for some reason."

"The hell with that. You better not leave your man and turn your back."

They both laughed.

Sophia sniffed a flower and stifled a sneeze.

"C'mon, I need to get out of here before I start sneezing my head off too."

The two women stepped out into the brightness of the afternoon. It was much warmer than Boston, but nice. The puffy clouds made the sky look like the walls of a daycare center.

There were a group of teenaged guys sitting in the car a few spaces from the one they arrived in. The music was loud and the bass sounded horrible—it had more scratch to it than boom. Sophia figured they were waiting for their buddy inside.

They leaned against the rental car Candice was driving and watched the people walk by on the sidewalk. There was a Cajun restaurant on the right and a tattoo shop to the left of the florist.

What an eclectic group of businesses, Sophia thought. She saw a dance studio about a block away and thought about walking there to take a look in the window, but just leaned against the car instead.

"I like him a lot, Alex."

"I know." She stated the words without sarcasm or condescension. "He likes you too."

Sophia watched a kid jump the curb with a skateboard. She didn't turn to look at Alex when she said, "He told me he loves me."

"Oh?"

"Yes. He wants a relationship."

"And you don't?"

Sophia didn't answer for such a long time that Alex didn't think she would.

"I do." She played with the tips of her nails.

"Then what's the problem?"

"Family means the world to Ethan." Sophia looked up at Alex. "You know that; you heard his story."

"Yes, *and…*"

"I wouldn't be able to give him the family he wants." She looked away again. "I can't have children." She whispered.

"I'm sorry, Sophia."

"There's nothing to be sorry about, I've come to terms with it, but how can I be in a committed relationship when I'm not the whole package."

"Stop it!"

Sophia was startled by Alex's response.

"What?"

Alex turned to face Sophia. "I may have just found out Ethan is a Phoenix, but I *know* the Phoenix men and you are underestimating yours."

Was he really hers?

"Ethan was adopted. Do you really think he has to have a kid from his loins to love it?" Sophia squinted at the word "loins."

Who still says that?

Adopt a kid.

The thought had never occurred to her.

Adopt a kid… She toyed with the idea in her head a few moments and thought of Bridgett.

A little voiced asked sagely, "Could you really trust another man with her heart?"

She had once, and the heartbreak nearly killed her. Sophia knew she needed to try to put that hurt away.

Not normally the hugging type, she reached over and hugged her friend. They both smiled.

"How long do you think they'll be in there?" Sophia asked Alex.

"I don't know. It could take a while. Ms. Lula has a story about each flower."

"Take a walk with me down to the dance studio. I just want to peek inside."

"Ok."

Pausing briefly to look inside the window of the tattoo business, they headed towards the dance studio. Sophia stopped suddenly and looped her arm through Alex's to get her to stop as well. They were about twenty feet away from the door of the studio. Her heart beat wildly and a silent alarm screamed in her head.

"What's wrong?" Alex asked, looking at Sophia then at the man she was staring at. "What is it, Soph?"

"That man," She whispered. "He looks like the man who's been stalking me."

Chapter 21

Unexpected Arrivals

A short stocky man with dark hair and balding, was holding the door open for a lady exiting the dance studio.

Still holding on to Alex's arm, Sophia turned quickly and began walking back to the flower shop.

"Are you sure, Soph?" Alex asked, trying to keep up with her friend's steps.

"It looked like him."

"But what would he be doing in Baton Rouge?"

Sophia slowed and looked at her friend.

"You're right. I'm getting paranoi—" Before she could get the word "paranoid" out of her mouth, a strong hand grabbed her upper arm and she felt a tiny pinch sting her neck. She was yanked free from Alex and stumbled from the sudden movement.

Alex screamed.

The man was not much taller than she, but he was much stronger. The strap broke on her sandal which caused her to stumble again trying to regain her footing. A mixture of garlic, coffee and stale cigarettes assaulted her nose when he tried to pull her into an embrace.

Sophia tried to still the fear racing through her veins threatening to numb her.

She had to think.

What had she learned in her self-defense classes to get out of this kind of attack? But she couldn't think. Everything was cloudy and her tongue felt too large for her mouth. Before she could wonder where Alex could be or scream for help, though her thick tongue threatened to make it impossible, a hand was slapped over her mouth.

"Keep still my love. I've come to take you home." She felt his erection pressed against her stomach. She thought of her friend Kristina and bile rose to the back of her throat.

Sophia kicked wildly, refusing to be a victim, but the force of her kicks were lacking and the effort seemed to enrage him further.

Ethan flashed in her mind—his face, his thick eyebrows, dark eyes, his ebony curly hair, and heart-melting smile. She needed to get back to him. She needed to feel his arms enfold her. She needed to hear his voice. She needed to dance with him.

She needed *him*.

This man could not have her. She forced a scream that would not come. Her arms ached where he held on firmly to them, but she had to get free.

273

Think Sophia…think! Just as she was about to sink her teeth into his oily skin she heard it.

Click.

It seemed to echo much too loudly in her head.

"Let her go." A voice commanded.

Blinded by fury, she couldn't see the person who owned the voice, though she was released immediately.

She fell to the sidewalk, her legs unable to support her. She looked up into a haze of faces and found herself surrounded by the young teens from the car near the flower shop. One had a gun to Julian's head; another pulled her up slowly, not taking his eyes off the man.

Alex ran over and pulled her away from the men. Thank God Alex was safe, she thought. Feeling heavy and disoriented, her legs shook so fiercely she was barely able to stand on her own. She leaned against the wall of a store unable to focus on the people gawking at her.

Deep breaths…deep breaths…she thought.

She needed to calm herself. She gulped in the air, freeing her nostrils from the pungent odor of the man that left a foul taste on her tongue.

When she could remember how to stand, she took in the scene.

A young African-American teen held a black pistol to Julian's head. Julian's soulless black eyes bore into hers and then suddenly, a strange, faintly eager look flashed in them. It made her skin crawl.

She tried to focus on the sirens she heard in distance, but the bear's roar was much too loud. She saw Alex's mouth moving and Candice and Chelsea running towards them.

She saw them...

Then nothing.

Was he going to have to cuff her to his wrist to keep her out of trouble?

Ethan paced the hospital room, unable to believe what happened. That bastard literally tried to take her off of the street in broad daylight.

He'd been out with Joshua, Landon and Terry when he received a phone call from the private detective. Julius Crankton had been traced to Baton Rouge. He'd used a credit card to check into a hotel room that morning. Ethan had disconnected the call and was in the process of calling Sophia when Landon's cell rang. It was Candice informing them about the attack.

The tranquilizer he'd injected into her neck could have easily taken down two grown men twice her size; nevertheless the doctors said she would be fine. They gave her some medicine to counteract the tranquilizer, but said she still may feel sluggish for a few days.

Ethan felt like he was having déjà vu. Hadn't he just gone through this with her in Boston? Except this time, they knew who'd poisoned her.

Alex was fine. She was a little shaken at first but when she saw the teens been arrested for possession of a firearm, she headed straight to the police station. Ethan was sure she would find a way to get the boys out of jail. Hell, he'd volunteered to pay any bail if needed.

"Hey, Baby. How're you feeling?" Ethan asked when he saw Sophia's eyes struggle to open.

He chuckled softly and shook his head. "What am I going to do with you?"

"Whatever you want." She mumbled. "I'm fine." She opened and closed her mouth making smacking sounds. "I'm thirsty."

He kissed her tenderly on her forehead. "Ok. I'll get you something to drink."

"How 'bout an orange freeze pop?" She asked and gave him a weak smile. "May as well keep the tradition going."

"Ok, Love. I will see what I can do, but this is a tradition I want to give up."

His fingers combed through her hair for a few moments before he tore himself away to leave the room.

"Be right back." He called softly over his shoulder.

The nurses' station was down the hall on the opposite end from Sophia's room.

He passed a few opened doors and felt haunted by some the eyes that followed him. They looked lonely—expectant. Maybe they were waiting for someone to visit them.

He hated hospitals. He made damn sure his mom's eyes never roamed the hallways waiting for someone to visit. He was always there.

"Ethan Powers." A stern voice came from behind him freeing him from the memory.

Ethan turned. It was Jocelyn Phoenix.

"Mrs. Phoenix?" His surprise was evident.

"I need to speak to you." She looked around and pulled her shoulders in as if germs were climbing the walls. "I prefer the coffee house across the street." She commanded.

Ethan didn't move. How could he? He watched her walk away.

Jocelyn turned back with questioning eyes, as if surprised he wasn't following.

"I meant right now."

Ethan raised a brow, but didn't move.

A nurse pushed an elderly lady in a wheel chair, crooning to her softly a long forgotten lullaby. Ethan watched how Jocelyn didn't try to mask her displeasure. Clearly everyone who was weak enough to be in a hospital was beneath her.

She stressed the words, pausing after each as if he was a bit slow. "I said I need to speak to you."

"I heard you the first time." This woman was the person who gave birth to him; the person who gave him up…she hadn't wanted him and now she wanted him to go with her to a coffee shop. "I'm sorry, but I'm unavailable to speak with you at the moment."

Her pale face was hard and serious. Ethan looked for a hint of softening in her eyes. There was none. Surely she knew by now who he was. For God's sakes, she was his mother and she looked at him as if she was commanding the gardener to use mulch with a better consistency of manure.

Jocelyn brushed a hand over her hair as if there was one that had strayed from the perfectly position bun at the nape of her neck. The black suit she wore was just as severe as the bun. The skirt was trimmed with the exact shade of the lime green purse that dangled from her wrist.

And were those gloves she clutched in her tiny hands?

The only women he'd seen wearing gloves on a warm day were the ladies in the royal family.

"It's urgent." She stated with a sense of authority.

"I don't doubt that." He replied flatly.

She glared at him, passed the gloves from one hand to the other and lifted her chin.

"When will you be available?"

"In about twenty minutes."

"Fine." The word sliced through the hallway— through him.

She left with the sounds of her heels echoing in her wake.

Ethan continued to the nurses' station with a million questions swirling in his mind.

They didn't have any ice pops so he returned with an orange soda and crushed ice.

"What did she want?" Sophia asked Ethan when he told her who he'd run into in the hallway.

"I don't know. She wants to meet me across the street."

She placed the soda on the tray hovering over the bed. "Are you going to meet her?" Her voice was soft.

"I don't know." He replied, mirroring her tone. "All my life I've been rehearsing what I would say to her if I got the chance." He looked absently at the cup and scratched a line into the foam. "Every time I did, I had something different to say." He looked up at Sophia. "I don't know what to say to her…I don't know what she wants."

She reached for him. He leaned over as she gently caressed his face and gave him a kiss. "Go talk to her."

She was wiping the table at the spot where she sat, clearly disgusted by being in such a place. The coffee shop appeared to be a favorite of the hospital employees. The majority of the patrons were in scrubs of various colors and designs. It wasn't crowded but many of the tables were taken because there were so few. Most of the customers, he assumed, sat at the counter where they could watch the barristers at work. Jocelyn Phoenix was not a "counter" type of woman. The music was low but lively. She stuck out like a green apple on a pile of coals.

"What do you want to talk about, Mrs. Phoenix?" Ethan stood at the table looking down at her.

Without looking at him she waved a hand and gestured for him to sit down.

"Sit."

Irritation clamped his jaws, but he sat in the chair across from her anyway.

"How much?"

Confused, he lifted a brow. "Excuse me?"

"How much are you after?"

Ethan straightened in his chair.

"I'm sorry, I don't follow."

She stirred her coffee and placed the spoon on a folded napkin next to the cup.

"Do you mind if I speak plainly?"

"Please." He said.

"You are a business man, yes?"

"Yes."

"All the decisions I've made in my life were for a specific purpose."

"What does business have to do with what you want to talk about?"

"Everything, Ethan."

Besides the moment in the hospital, this was the very first time she'd said his name. The first time for sure that she'd addressed him so casually. Was this some sort of apology? The best she knew how?

She continued. "I made a mistake with you, however."

Ethan stiffened. He hadn't expected this.

"How so?"

"Look at you." She smiled and the hairs rose on his neck. "You're successful and smart."

Ethan was taken aback. Speechless. Did she regret her decision? Her words hinted that she may have, but his gut tightened in warning.

"I was in love with Cortland, but knew I could never marry him." He'd known that from the letters. "But when I found out I was pregnant, I knew I had to act quickly." She waved her hand. "Well you know the rest, don't you?"

"Unfortunately, yes."

"It was not personal, just smart business. I was from a wealthy family. It was bad enough that I allowed myself to succumb to Cortland's charms, but my parents wouldn't have allowed such a match.

"Could it have been that he didn't want you?"

"He was a dreamer. I was too good for him." She spat out bitterly. She looked around to make sure no one was listening to them. "So, I ask again. How much do you want?"

"For what?"

"Clearly you are trying to extort money from Dixon, which is forcing him into a divorce. I take it you want the portion of the business you feel is rightfully yours?"

"Extortion?"

"Well, yes…It's always about business." She slid the cup to the side, with no intentions of drinking the coffee. "Do you know what a divorce will do to the business?"

"And you think you can pay me off?" He asked in an exasperated tone. This woman was a piece of work. "For what exactly?"

"Your silence of course."

"What do you think I have to say?"

"I am not your mother." She stated coolly. The statement told Ethan that when she delivered him, she'd severed any ties to him whatsoever and not once had she thought about the baby she'd thrown away.

"That, ma'am…is the first thing we can agree on." Ethan stood. "No, you are not my mother…and for that, I should be paying *you*." He stood next to her, leaned over and said, "Trust me; there is no way in hell I would want anyone to know you gave birth to me."

Jocelyn sat stoically in her chair as Ethan walked out of the coffee shop.

Seductive Pleasures

The moment he stepped onto the sidewalk he gulped the air to slow his pulse and keep the nausea at bay. He'd done it. He'd finally done it. Ethan had faced Jocelyn Phoenix. He'd confronted the demons of his past.

He felt relieved that he had not been raised by that woman. She didn't have a heart, which was sorely apparent. He was glad that his brothers were nothing like her. How had they escaped the shards of ice that fell from her everywhere she went?

From his talk with Dixon, he'd not really played a huge role in his sons' lives. So it must have been Cortland. My father, he thought, was such a man that he could mold his nephews into great men. Ethan wasn't as impressed that Cortland could do it, but rather that he did, in spite of Jocelyn. For the first time in his life he was proud to be a Phoenix. Despite Jocelyn's bitter attitude about him, he wanted to know more about Cortland Phoenix, his father.

Chapter 22

Sparrow

When Ethan returned to Sophia's hospital room she was asleep. He sat the bowl of soup he'd purchased for her on the rolling tray she'd pushed to the side. The television was on and two women were screaming at each other about someone leaving the milk out. It was one of those reality shows he hated.

Ethan turned off the TV and pulled out his phone to check his email. He'd been gone from the office for several days and the mail had piled up. He'd gone through about thirty emails when he slid his phone back into his pocket. Leaning his head back on the chair, he closed his eyes.

"Sparrow was my daughter." He turned quickly and went to her when he heard her tiny voice from the bed.

"Phia."

"I loved her. She was my baby…my everything. It took seventeen hours for her to arrive. There were complications. She was my first and last baby." He said nothing. "I loved her." She repeated. "My husband, Manuel." Her eyes closed and a tear slipped from the corner. Ethan brushed it with his thumb. "I loved him too. We married young; he was the love of my life and I was his. There was nothing he wouldn't do for me."

She didn't speak for a long time and Ethan wondered if she'd drifted back to sleep. He hadn't known she'd been married and he found himself wondering what type of man Manuel was.

"We had Sparrow and things began to change. He was jealous of the time I spent with her instead of him." More tears. "She was a baby." The words were a hoarse cry.

"Not now, Honey." He whispered. "Rest now."

But she continued.

"I tried to explain that to him over and over, but it was like something cracked inside of him. He was no longer my Manuel." She wiped the tears streaming onto the pillow. "He was…" She shook her head as if she still didn't understand. "I didn't feel safe leaving the baby with him. I had to sometimes stay up all night long, just to make sure he didn't harm her."

"Did you go to the police?" He asked gently.

A terse laugh erupted from her throat.

"Little good did that do. They said there was nothing they could do if there was no physical evidence of abuse…basically they couldn't do anything on a hunch."

Ethan pulled a tissue from the table next to the bed and wiped her face. She pushed his hand away with so much force it startled him.

His eyes rounded when he witnessed the pain distorting the features of her face. His heart broke watching her relive her grief.

"It's my fault. I couldn't keep her safe." She sobbed.

"No baby." He breathed the words into a whisper.

"I dozed off for a moment and he took her." She looked up into Ethan's sad eyes. "He took my baby, Ethan… and…" She choked on her sobs.

Being careful of the IV line in her arm he climbed into bed behind her and held her close. She'd probably never voiced her grief before and needed to get it out.

"He drove into a ravine with her in the car."

Ethan wrapped his arms and legs around her, trying to absorb some of the pain that he knew would never leave her.

"He took my baby from me."

"What happened to Manuel?" He had to know.

"He's dead…I wish I'd killed him." He could feel her shaking. "He survived the crash but when he was released from the hospital, finally tried and sentenced to prison, he didn't survive the first night."

"Someone killed him?"

"The reports said he was accidently stabbed during a prison riot."

"You didn't believe the reports."

"No."

"Why not?"

"He was stabbed thirteen times." She paused. "Later the coroner told me he was already dead when he was stabbed. The evidence proved he'd been suffocated."

Neither of them said anything for a long time.

What *could* you say after that?

"Manuel told me he loved me…that he was in love with me."

Ethan's heart fell.

This was the point when she told him she was too damaged to love again or to trust anyone.

"But you are not Manuel." Her small voice filled him.

"No. I'm not." He tried to keep his voice steady.

"You're Ethan."

He loved the way she said his name.

"Yes."

288

"And you love me."

"Yes I do." He pulled her into him.

"Ok."

"Ok?"

"Yes, I will let you."

Epilogue

The Beginning

"How're you feeling, Baby?"

It still felt strange to hear Ethan call her that, but it made her feel all squishy inside.

She smiled. "I'm fine." And she was. She had a surprisingly quick recovery after the attack, which could have been helped along by Alex and Candice invading her room for a private spa day.

The wedding was beautiful. No one would have ever known the mother of the bride suffered a stroke so recently or that one of the bridesmaids was released from the hospital only hours before the wedding.

Mrs. Lillian Carwin was almost as beautiful as the bride in her emerald green floor length gown. However, all anyone had to do was look into Landon's eyes when Mr. Carwin escorted his daughter down the aisle to know he only had eyes for Candice.

Candice was stunning. Her dark skin glowed against the cream colored beaded gown. She and Landon complimented each other so well. There was no way anyone could look at them and not feel the happiness and love shining from them.

Dixon Phoenix sat proudly on the front row watching his son declare his love to Candice, and Jocelyn Phoenix sat next to him as if they were the ideal couple. She'd arrived only moments before the wedding began. She, however, was not seen at the reception. Oddly enough, no one noticed her absence, or if they did, they didn't care.

"Are you ready?"

Sophia stuffed the last of her things that could possibly fit into her suitcase. She lift her eyes and stared at the dress hanging on the back of the bedroom door along with the delicate shoes placed so carefully back in their box and bag, hanging on the door knob. She knew Ethan's question held more than it seemed on the surface. It was a simple enough, but there were so many other questions that spiked from it that it was anything but.

Was she ready?

Landon and Candice left for their honeymoon immediately after the wedding and the other house guests soon after. Ethan and she were the last two in the house. It felt kind of odd to be in the house alone. It felt so empty and she would miss almost everyone. She'd especially become closer to Alex. Chelsea, thank goodness had bid farewell soon after the wedding reception.

Terry had some unfinished business in Florida, before he headed back to Boston. And since the threat of Julian was gone, Erika was free to return to New York. Sophia wondered if there would be a love match between the two, but Terry had rebuffed all of Erika's advances and any other woman's that he'd encountered.

Sophia had asked Landon a little about him and why he appeared to be a little aloof at times. Landon was convinced he was still in love with a woman he'd met in college, which made her suspect that was the unfinished business.

She turned to Ethan and gave him an exasperated smile.

"I'm not ever going to fit all this stuff in here."

"You knew that when you bought all that stuff."

Somehow shooting him the universal "fuck you" sign seemed a little harsh, but oh how she wanted to.

She tried not to roll her eyes and shot him a look instead. It was hopeless because that damn smile of his knew how to wiggle its way between her resolve and whatever traitorous place that linked to her heart…and other parts.

"I'm going to need another bag unless I ship the rest." She said struggling to zip the suitcase.

"Where will you ship it?"

There it was.

The first spike…

What to do about their relationship once they left Baton Rouge.

She sat on the bed, crossed her legs and watched his eyes follow the movement.

"Ethan, you knew I had to go home at some point. You can't take care of me forever."

As soon as the words slipped off her tongue she wished she could retrieve them.

Too late.

"That's exactly what I'd planned to do."

The intensity of his gaze caught her off guard. She'd seen the look before—raw, vulnerable and… sincere.

Yesterday, at the wedding while holding the bouquet of flowers tightly in her hands to keep from dropping them because she was so aware of him, she'd felt the way his eyes spoke to her when Landon and Candice recited their vows.

Promise filled them; heat ignited them and seduction called her.

The same reaction that overtook her then was over taking her now. Her heartbeat sped. Passion tickled the bottom of her feet, spread its fingers and inched up the back of her legs. She couldn't stop it then and she damn sure couldn't stop it now. The pulse at the juncture of her thighs beckoned him like a sirens call. She squeezed her legs tightly to stop it, but still he came.

Ethan took a step towards her.

No. She closed her eyes and shook her head slowly.

She had to put a stop to this.

Sophia stood.

"Ethan." She whispered; her voice unusually thick with her accent.

He did not stop.

"Yes?" He voice husky and undeterred.

"I thought you were ready to go."

"I don't have anywhere to be."

There was no time to say anything else, because the moment she opened her mouth to say whatever useless rebuttal that would come to mind, he'd captured her mouth with his and all thoughts dissolved into a fissure of desire.

This man. This man. This man.

She could not get enough of this man. She could not get enough of Ethan Powers.

Suddenly like the loud clang of symbols, she realized he was offering her as much as she wanted of him. He could be all hers.

With the palm of her hands pressed flat on his chest, she felt his heartbeat. It was fast, steady and strong. It made her feel alive. Her arms slipped easily around his neck as she pressed herself into him.

His erection was hard with promise. She needed him—had to have him…here…now. She needed him to fill her.

"Love me, Ethan." Her voice was such a strangled cry that she vaguely recognized it.

In reply, he slipped the straps of her peach top off her shoulders. The heat of his breath seared her neck as he plied kisses along it.

Sensual pleasure moistened her folds.

"Pleeeaase, Ethan." She groaned.

With deft hands, Ethan unfastened the buckle of his belt, unbuttoned his pants and made quick work of the zipper. Before he could pull himself free, Sophia reached inside his pants and took him in her hand. With a solid grip and a slow stroke she gloried in the velvety smooth feeling of his full erection.

"Phia." Her name slid from his lips. "Baby, if you want me to fill you," he gritted, "you better stop that."

Her eyes peeked up at him as she lifted the corner of her mouth in a wicked grin. Her hands moved in a slow cadence that mimicked the one that beat at her core.

She knew and he knew that this slow sweet seduction would be the undoing of them both.

Boston two months later:

He was nervous, though he was unsure why. He'd seen her almost every day for the past two months. At first he told himself it was because she was recovering from the hospital, but that lie only worked for about a week or so. Then he made himself believe he showed up every evening to see if she'd gotten the results of her tests. It had been over a month since the night they drove to the Frozen Cow to celebrate her negative results with ice cream; so he could no longer ride on the coattails of that pretentious excuse.

Now, there were no excuses; he simply wanted to see her. Dixon pressed the glowing button and waited. His hand shook when he heard the click of the lock so he gripped the large envelope in his hand a little tighter.

"Hello Dixon." She smiled as she stepped aside to let him in. "I wasn't expecting you...Come in."

He stepped inside and admired the soft pink dress she wore. It fit snug on her small waist and plunged a bit exposing just a hint of cleavage. The color seemed to make the tiny gold flecks in her green eyes stand out even more. Damn she's beautiful he thought.

"Have a seat."

Dixon took a deep breath, walked towards the sofa and sat. "I'm sorry for dropping in on you...again." He smiled at the last word because his drop-ins were becoming a habit. "You look as if you're going out. Am I interrupting your evening?"

"No. I just felt like wearing this today." She sat on the sofa next to him. "What's going on? You came back for another whipping in spades?"

Many of the evenings they spent together, they played board games or cards. Something he'd never done before. Neither ever spoke about all the time they spent together and what it meant. But tonight, he felt it was about time they did.

Gloria saw the large manila envelope.

"Do you have something I need to go over for a client?"

He looked at the envelope on his lap. "Not exactly."

She frowned and appraised him, noticing for the first time that he appeared nervous.

"Everything ok?" Before he could answer she asked, "Oh, how did it go with that creep who attacked Sophia?"

"Sentenced to twenty-five years in prison."

"And those young boys that pulled the gun out on him?"

"Alex got all the charges dropped long ago.

"That's wonderful. That was ashamed that they were even charged at all. Those boys were heroes. I hate to think what would've happened to Sophia if they hadn't intervened."

"I know. But Alex refused to leave Baton Rouge until all the charges were dropped…It didn't take long. She's relentless."

He rubbed his hands together.

"What is it, Dixon?"

"Gloria…I…uh…"

She frowned. "Dixon Phoenix are you trying to fire me."

"In a sense, yes."

298

"What!" She'd been kidding.

Dixon pulled out a few documents from the envelope. She frowned again. She usually saw every document that landed in Dixon's hands; however she'd never seen the ones he laid on her coffee table.

He pointed at the set of papers closest to her. "These are the documents that give my company to my sons."

She put her hand to her chest. "Dixon!...Why?"

"It's time for me to retire, Gloria. There are some things I want to do. So I have divided the company three ways. Each of my boys with an equal part."

"Three?" She asked still not quite believing that he was giving up the reins of his empire.

"Yes. Landon, Joshua and Ethan." He saw her smile and nod of approval and it made him feel good about his decision. "I know that technically Ethan is my nephew, but Cortland took care of my boys like they were his own...Who am I to do any less?"

She reached up and gently slid her hand along his shoulder.

"So, I'm out of a job?" She asked with a tinge of concern.

"I'm sure the boys won't get rid of any employees."

"What about Joshua?"

"Joshua is leaving the everyday running of things to Landon, Ethan and their cousin, Terry, while he and Alex try to figure out where they want to live long term. They're enjoying sailing around on the Phoenix right now."

She could tell what the second set of documents was, but waited for his explanation.

"These are my divorce papers. It was final today."

"So soon."

"It was uncontested."

Gloria raised a brow.

"It was to my good fortune that she is so pretentious and shallow. She didn't want the truth about Ethan to be dragged through the courts."

"How do *you* feel about Ethan?"

"Grateful to know the truth, otherwise I never would've been able to get away from Jocelyn without a long drawn out battle. There was no way I could continue with the charade of a marriage we were living." He looked at her long and hard. "It would've been over even if I hadn't found out about Ethan."

"I'm sorry, Dixon."

"Don't be. I'm not."

"How is Ethan adjusting to his new family?"

"There really is no difference. The boys have always treated him like a brother and they have no problem letting everyone know that he's Cortland's son." Dixon's smile softened. "People are just thinking his mom, Janice, and Cortland were an item at one time and they aren't saying any differently...Oh yea...Sophia finally agreed to marry him."

"That's wonderful. They've found some good women to be by their sides."

He reached for the last set of papers. "Which brings me to this." He picked them up and turned towards her so he could see her clearly.

"What's that?" She asked softly.

"This is a deed to a house I bought off the coast of South Carolina. It's on the beach, large porch and a no neighbors."

"A secluded home on the beach is a rare find."

"Yes, but..."

"But what?" Her eyes did not leave his.

"I need someone to share it with?"

"I love the beach."

"I was hoping."

Dixon tossed the papers towards the table and did what he'd wanted to do for years, but didn't because he wanted her to know he was a man of honor. He'd hated his life, disliked his wife and was completely miserable at home, but until he was free from it all, he knew he couldn't be the man he wanted to be to Gloria. He pulled her into his arms and claimed her with a kiss full of promise.

His Gloria.

Finally, he could truly be happy.

Dear Reader,

Thank you, thank you for taking this journey with me. I hope you've fallen as madly in love with the Phoenix men as I have. *Seductive Pleasures* is the final novel in The Pleasures Collection, but I'm not absolutely sure you won't meet the Phoenix's again.

Who knows...

You can find the entire collection in the book titled, Simple Surrendered Seduction.

For all of you who have encouraged me with your kind words, you have no idea how much you are appreciated.

Sincerely,

Natasha Simmons